OFFSPRING

OFFSPRING

by E.J. ROSTEN

Manuscript by Julie O'Connell

Published in the United States by Relium Media LLC.
www.angelpunksaga.com

ISBN-13: 978-0-9853521-4-1

*The Divine Beings cohabited with the daughters of men,
who bore them Offspring.
They were the heroes of old, the men of renown.*

Genesis 6:4

Prologue

*I*stanbul *never seems to age, it simply adapts to survive,* thought Momar Singh as he surveyed the ancient city's skyline. The minarets of the Hagia Sophia, the dome of the Blue Mosque, and the hills surrounding the bay were all postcard perfect. Hardly a ripple on the river meant the fishing boat was steady and even as it docked under a forbidding stone cliff.

Before stepping off the bow, Momar made the tiniest of adjustments to his turban, brushed off dust particles no one could see, and made one last pass over his beard. If he was sure of anything on this perilous errand, he knew appearing unkempt in the High Council Chamber would not do. He glanced up at the immense camel-colored walls and tower at the apex of the cliff, the ancient stones concealing so much beauty, so much power.

After paying the fisherman a few coins, he stepped onto the dock. The small buildings around the water were humble and simple, yet tidy. He squared his shoulders and strode carefully up the path that led to the outlying edge of the High Council fortress.

A plain steel gate was inset into the stone, the simplicity of the metalwork was precisely the reason no one ever noticed it. Behind the gate stood a figure dressed in blood-red robes, his face obscured by the drape of a hood. As Momar approached, the gold symbols embroidered down the front of the scarlet robes caught his eye, the threadwork glistening in the morning sun.

The hooded man—Momar knew him to be a Crimson Scribe—slipped the hood down onto his shoulders. "I am Ginju. Armaros is waiting," he said as he swung the gate open.

Momar knew of Ginju, one of the oldest and most senior of the Crimson Scribes, but had never met him. The man's bald head was ringed with a pattern of tattoos, many matching the symbols on his robe. Momar had always found tattoo choices fascinating, though he knew these particular symbols had everything to do with the man's calling and powerful position, rather than an artistic decision.

Momar followed Ginju into the keep. They passed through a few hallways and rooms, all connected and each one grander and more imposing than the last. Every time Momar had been here he'd wanted to stop and admire the intricate details, but he'd always had an errand or a specific purpose that kept him from lingering. Today was no different—one did not ignore one's guide, especially when one was to meet Armaros.

After passing through a final courtyard, they stood before huge, multistory double doors, one slightly ajar enabling him to see into the chamber itself. Ginju indicated with a simple hand motion that Momar was to enter. Momar nodded once and gave a small bow of gratitude, then stepped inside.

The council chamber never failed to send a chill down his back; the enormity of the room made him aware of how small humans were, while the craftwork of the place made him proud of what humans could accomplish. A shaft of golden light from the oculus opening at the zenith of the marble dome overhead illuminated a raised throne dais. An older woman, her silver hair braided and falling down her back, knelt before the largest of twelve thrones. Seated on this central throne, was a life-sized marble statue, but the sculpture's body was obscured by massive wings folded around itself. Eleven slightly smaller and empty thrones fanned out to either side.

As Momar stepped deeper into the cavernous space, he could see the woman's face was upturned and that she rested one hand on the wing of the seated stone figure.

The woman cocked her head slightly to one side. "Momar."

He bowed. "Armaros." He imparted as much respect and honor as he could into the one word.

Armaros rose, touched her forehead once before she turned to him, gracefully stepping down from the dais to his level. "And how is the Layil child?"

"Two years old. Healthy." He hesitated a bit and cleared his throat. "Precocious." Nothing else needed to be said.

"Very good." Armaros looked into Momar's eyes. "Your visit is quite unusual, but unfortunately, I don't think there is another way."

She shook her head.

"Anything that will help me keep her alive is worth doing. As the Layil Scribe, it is my sworn duty." Momar made a small inclination of his head, deferring to Armaros and her position.

She raised one eyebrow. "I am well aware of your duties. This, however, will be dangerous. You may not learn enough, and I fear for what you may reveal. Are you prepared for the Twins to probe your mind?"

He nodded. "I am as prepared as I can be." He couldn't think of any adequate way to fully ready oneself for being sent outside the human concept of time—he was human, after all.

"Very well. We will begin." Without another word, Armaros took a step closer to Momar and placed her hands on his shoulders. He closed his eyes, waiting for the transfer. Light and warmth flooded his being.

Momar stood on golden sand, nothing else around him as far as he could see. A brisk wind stirred the sand and brought his attention back to himself. The wind picked up intensity, forcing him to wipe the granules from his eyes.

The sand began to shift and assemble itself into a rectangular shape. Billions of grains poured upward as if looking at an hourglass in reverse. In a second or two, a full-sized mosque built of sand appeared. But as he moved forward, it crumbled to nothing with his first step. Then the sand built itself into a monastery, then a cathedral, then a Greek temple—the structure changing with each of his measured footfalls as he drew ever closer.

In the end, the temple shape remained. Momar walked through

an opening into an open courtyard. At the other end of the sandy expanse were two large thrones, each draped with a glowing, pearlescent figure. As he continued his approach, the walls of the courtyard and the surrounding temple melted away. Now only the two figures remained seated on their thrones, an adolescent girl and boy, and him.

The girl asked, "Are you human?" Although she was unclothed, her hair covered her like a robe. Everything about her glowed, including her all-white eyes.

Momar nodded and bowed slightly. While his breathing seemed to have increased, he couldn't feel his heartbeat. He swallowed once and tried to maintain his outward calm.

Then the boy asked, "And how is it a human can step outside of time?" He too was clad only in his own hair, and his eyes narrowed as he spoke.

"I am a Scribe. The Offspring family I serve sent me here to seek what only you may know." He bowed again.

Both figures queried in unison, as they sat up, "WHY?"

Momar could both see and feel their irritation blended with something akin to a cruel curiosity. Momar's body moved back a step as if pushed by an invisible hand. There was so much danger here—so many paths that could go horribly wrong. "There is a child I ..."

The Twins rose as one. Momar could feel them both in his mind, the pain building in his head. They demanded together, "She's not just any child, is she?"

They raised both of their arms toward Momar. "You. Will. Show. Us ..."

The pain in his skull approached blackout level. His knees buckled and his hands went to his head—the agony singular in its intensity. Visions flashed through his mind—a large gathering of First Born and Offspring, a man in a hood with a huge sword, and twining cords of metal enveloping a body. He heard the wailing of a woman and the screams of children. Having the Twins in his mind was a link of sorts, and he felt every mote of their anger, their sadness, their sense of longing. Danger, peril, jeopardy, menace— it was all of them and it was all-encompassing.

The Twins screamed, "... Show ... Us ... EVERYTHING!"

ONE

Guards restraining her arms, blood seeping from her lip, and rain pissing down outside—Mara shook her head at the insanity of it all. *Another day in freaking paradise.*

"They jumped me. You know it. I know it," she said in an even voice. Juvie guard-ladies did not appreciate hysterics or screaming or swearing. She looked over at one of the girls sprawled on the floor and nodded in that direction. The same way she would have recited boring poetry, she said, "I was just doing my job, cooking the eggs. She smacked me in the face with a pan." She had also said many inappropriate words that slurred Mara's parents, intellect, and mental state, but it would have been a colossal waste of time to bring it up.

One inmate on the floor sat up with her hand on her cheek, and glared at Mara, her gaze promising payback of the worst kind. "She lies. Never touched her. We were all just putting things away."

Mara rolled her eyes and shook her head. "No, they were not, and I'm not lying. You think I split my own lip?" She dabbed at it with her tongue.

The guard on Mara's right side said, "Enough. Let's go, Layil." She pulled Mara toward the doorway, the other guard following suit. A third guard pointed to the mess on the stovetop and said to the other gawking inmates, "Clean that up and go about your business."

Two girls in bright orange jumpsuits stepped forward to do as the guards had instructed, one to the smoking eggs on the grill, one to the pots and pans scattered across the floor. Neither made eye contact with Mara as she was escorted out of the kitchen. *Which was exactly as it should have been.*

At least the guards were pulling her along almost in step this time. It was always a challenge to have one side yanked forward, then the other. Made her feel like a toddler just learning to walk. The last thing Mara heard before the kitchen door slammed shut behind her was one of the girls on the floor saying, "Enjoy solitary, blond bitch." There were mumbled profanities after that, pitched low so the guards couldn't hear. And so many threats.

Mara heard every word.

It really was a magical place.

Once through the door, the guards loosened their death-grip on her arms just a tad bit and Mara said, "Really, I know the drill. I can walk on my own." Solitary confinement was a blessing in this hellhole. Sometimes she broke the rules just to get a little peace and quiet. Sure, the meals in confinement were even worse than the cafeteria, if that was possible, but no worse than doing a cleanse in some expensive spa on the outside.

The cranky guard-ladies on either side of her ignored her and steered her down a different corridor. She looked from one to the other, her eyebrows knitted together in confusion. "Hey, I don't mean to tell you how to do your job or anything, but solitary is the other way." Mara couldn't help the words floating out and instantly kicked herself. The guards here didn't care that the inmates were young girls. Their nightsticks were not decorations, and their training included how to land a painful hit without leaving any visible marks.

Miss Right Guard said, "I know you're gonna miss the alone time, but it seems to be your lucky day, Layil." She tugged Mara's arm again.

Mara snorted a little. "Lucky? Scrubbing toilets with my own toothbrush is lucky?"

"Nope. Wrong again. You're being released. Two whole days early. We got a big delivery of new girls and we need the room, so we're booting your skinny ass out." Miss Left Guard chuckled a little bit.

They led Mara through another set of doors and into the dorm wing, stopping at Mara's bed. The guards dropped her arms. "You got five minutes to get your crap together. Meet us at the monitor station," Miss Right Guard said before both women turned on their heels and left the dormitory.

Home. *I'm going home.* She could see Max, and Momar, and Max, and Dadima, and Max, and Mick, and her baby ... she could ride her baby again. The smile that had crept onto her face crashed and burned. Because she'd also have to explain to Momar, in graphic and minute detail, everything that had happened inside juvie, and everything that had led up to her conviction.

Nobody has that kind of time.

Thinking of time made her jump. Five minutes? She only had five minutes! Mara dabbed at her lip a bit, wiping the blood on the sleeve of her jumpsuit. She reached into her cubby and pulled out everything she possessed, or everything the Cascadia Correctional Facility would let her possess. The sum total of her life here in paradise was a grayish towel, some skinny black flip-flops, her journal, and her pencil drawings. But her most treasured possession was a picture of Max on his last birthday. The cake in the pic was bigger than he was, and his grin a million times bigger than the cake. She smiled at the thought of being able to hug him in person sooner than she'd expected. *The little guy isn't all that little anymore.* He might complain when she gave his shaggy blond head the noogie it seriously needed.

"Excuse me, is this your spot?" A quiet voice interrupted her thoughts.

Mara's head snapped up. A petrified young face was looking at her, the girl's arms full of sheets, towels, and new flip-flops. "I was told this was my bunk." Mara felt the waves of terror coming off the newbie like rays of the sun.

"Out with the old, in with the new, right?" Mara laid out her towel and placed her things in the center, then wrapped it up into a bundle.

"Huh?" The new girl didn't seem to follow, which was the normal response to almost everything that came out of Mara's mouth.

Mara could have scared the bejeesus out of the girl but opted for honesty and kindness. *Do unto others, right?* She reached into her cubby and pulled out a battered copy of *Faces in the Water*. She placed it on top of the bunk. "Yeah, I know how you feel. This'll help you keep what's left of your sanity. Good luck. Keep your head down. And don't engage with any of the gang kids." She picked up her things and walked out of the dorm room.

If she never saw this place again, it would be too soon.

TWO

The line at the release door wasn't very long. There were two boys from the male side of the facility, and one girl Mara didn't recognize. The three of them eyed Mara up and down and then quickly looked away like she might give them eye cooties. Mara sat on one of the benches with her bundle clutched tightly to her chest. She touched her lip with her tongue again, feeling the slight swelling, and tasted the coppery tang of blood. Those damn kitchen girls—if she hadn't been going home, she'd have taught them a thing or two about fighting that would have scared them away for good. *Honestly, what kind of maniac attacks the person cooking everyone's breakfast?*

A buzz sounded, then the door opened, letting in a tall thin boy wearing yet another orange jumpsuit. Mara brightened and gave him a nod. He nodded back with a smile and sat next to her, then pointed to his mouth, "I see you're doing great with applying the lessons from group, huh?" He grinned, a little crooked and a lot adorable.

Mara smiled back, which split her lip again. "Ow. Dammit, Ethan. Yeah, I'm definitely on the 'needs work' list for anger management." She made an imaginary check mark in the air, then dabbed at her lip with the sleeve of her jumpsuit. Ethan Skylar had been the one person she'd been able to carry on a conversation with inside juvie—a bright spot in the otherwise soul-sucking world of Cascadia.

His smile didn't dim. "Hey, if it wasn't for your unique approach to group, I'm not sure I'd still be here." Mara pursed her lips together to stop the bleeding and to prevent the snicker from escaping. He'd been the one who'd kept *her* from trouble in group, when she'd wanted to bash in heads and scorch them all with sarcasm and her legendary biting wit. She shook her head, lips still pursed.

Another buzz sounded, and a guard came out. "Layil, it's your turn."

Mara stood up and looked down at Ethan. He said with a nod, "See you out front?"

She nodded back and walked through the doorway. On the other side, she approached a counter with a window, a uniformed guard standing opposite her holding a large plastic bag with her name on it. The guard inventoried each item as he laid it on the counter. "One pair boots, black. One pair tights, black. One skirt, black. One blouse, black. One denim jacket, black. One cell phone, black. One small handbag, black. And the handbag is empty." He raised one eyebrow and slid a piece of paper across to Mara. "Sign it."

The bag hadn't been empty when she'd been admitted, but the guard's expression dared her to do anything about it.

Mara rolled her eyes. She tucked her towel bundle under one arm and signed. *Whatever.*

It didn't take long for her to get dressed in the bathroom next to the release area. Even year-old clothes that hadn't been cleaned in forever were preferable to the uniform she'd had to wear inside. She felt more like herself than she had in months, and there was a little bit of sweetness seeing the damn orange jumpsuit in the trash. Orange was not the color to wear when your skin and hair were as pale as hers—made her look like a walking creamsicle.

Mara checked her reflection and turned a bit to see her back. The bony knobs on her shoulder blades she'd spent a lifetime ignoring or explaining? Still there, mocking her. But once she put her jacket on everything was covered. You'd never know anything was different.

Dressed in civvie clothes, it felt funny not to be wearing any makeup, but since her purse had been picked clean by the guards, she didn't have a lot of choice. Her cell phone was dead, but that wasn't a surprise. She finger-combed her hair, trying to get it to some semblance of the normal chunky spikes she preferred. Nope. Prison hair was her lot in life until she got home. It could be so much worse. She could be eating those burned eggs or scrubbing toilets or fighting those kitchen witches.

The exterior double door was on a motion sensor and opened with a whoosh as she approached. Secretly, she'd expected some kind of fanfare to celebrate getting out, but the reality was just a quiet nothing. The pick-up area for released kids was nonexistent and the rain was still bucketing down, not that it bothered her. She was a true Pacific Northwest girl, through and through. She let a few drops fall on her face. The air was sweeter and softer than she'd remembered.

She was out. She was OUT. She felt like painting her face blue and screaming, "Freedom!"

A group of people stood under umbrellas, some holding flowers or pets, waiting to take their freshly liberated inmates to waiting cars. Mara flattened herself against the wall under the eaves to stay dry-ish and looked around for someone she knew. Her heart beat a little faster. Could it be Mom or Dad picking her up? Were they back home? She shook it off and faced reality. If there had been good news about her parents, someone would have let her know.

"Sweet boots. Love all the buckles." Ethan sidled up next to her. "Honestly, I didn't know you were out today." His face beamed a little bit at his own freedom, and he couldn't stop smiling. Dressed in civilian clothes of jeans, hoodie, and a long black jacket, he looked both taller and skinnier than he had in his jumpsuit. His curly brown hair seemed to respond to the moisture in the air by getting curlier in the perfect way men's hair does, his face burnished with a hint of pink under the light-coffee color of his skin.

Mara remembered to breathe, then nodded. "Umm, yeah, news to me, too. Guess they had a new batch of delinquents banging at the door."

Ethan shook his head. "Tsk. Tsk. What's the world coming to?"

She smirked as much as her lip would allow. He gave her some side-eye and cleared his throat. "Umm, I know this is weird, but can I umm ... text you my number? I'd like ... umm ... you know ... we could ..." He hemmed and hawed for a couple of seconds, which was awesome.

Mara let him off the hook after a second or two of silence. "Got a pen?" He fished one out of his coat and handed it to her. "Give me your hand." She took his hand in hers, flipped it over, and wrote her cell number on his palm. "It's dead now, 'cause, you know, I just got it back, so give me a few hours, okay?" A warm feeling in her midsection traveled to her face, and she knew her cheeks had flushed. Another curse of ultra-fair skin.

Ethan smiled and began to say something, but he was interrupted by a loud rumble coming from the parking lot. Both of their heads swiveled, and they saw two enormous chopper-style motorcycles bookending a brand-new, immaculate Range Rover— one in front and one behind. "Whoa." Ethan's tone was suitably impressed.

Mara, however, rolled her eyes. "Oh. My. God. Really?" She'd wanted her family. But this was like the Layil circus arriving in town—with ginormous elephants, fireworks, and a marching band. The warmth from Ethan's attention dissipated and her skin crawled a little bit.

Ethan turned to look at her. "All that's for you? Wow. Nice entourage." His eyebrows were raised practically to his hairline, and his tone of voice seemed to indicate sarcasm.

Mara had been making excuses about her family all her life. She was damn tired of it and she'd expected better from him, of all people. She shook her head, her lips pressed together in a straight line that had little to do with reducing blood flow. She walked toward the now-parked car, dodging raindrops, then took a deep breath and stopped. It wasn't his fault. Ethan was impressed, not making fun. He *was* better than other people. She'd let her emotions steer the ship without checking with her brain. Mara took another deep breath and turned back. "You need a ride somewhere?"

Before he could answer, the door to the Range Rover opened, and a boy leaped out and splashed over to her, ignoring the puddles. Max wrapped himself around her like a giant python. Mara laughed as she gripped his small body to hers. "I can't believe you're eleven now!" she said. The blood sang in her veins, her heart almost bursting with love for the little poophead. She looked back at Ethan and said, "Do you? Need a ride? Come on ... we're getting soaked." Raindrops caught in her lashes, making everything seem sparkling.

Ethan shrugged and dashed over to where Mara and Max stood. "Yes, please."

There was the small pop of an umbrella opening next to the car. "Mara, who is this?" A deep melodic voice, one she'd often heard in her sleep, tickled her ears.

She blinked and the sparkly environment returned back to a dismal parking lot. Even though having him here was exactly what she'd expected, she'd hoped for a little more "honeymoon" time before the inquisition began. Mara turned to him and said, "Momar, we're just giving him a ride downtown. We've got room and he needs a ride. Max is fine with it, right?" Max nodded his head, still stuck to her like a limpet. She patted his back a few more times, every molecule in her body rejoicing in his presence.

"This is not a good time." Momar glared at her, his turban immaculate under the umbrella, his beard graying but neatly trimmed. No "hello." No "good to see you." No "did the evil bitches inside make every day a living hell." Just questions and orders, as usual.

Between gritted teeth, she said, "He's my friend, and he comes with us. It's just a few minutes out of our way, right?" Mara gestured toward the car. "We're not getting any drier." She felt drips falling onto her shoulders from her soggy hair.

Momar looked at Mara, then at Ethan, then back to Mara. "Get under the umbrella then," he grumbled. He held it so it sheltered the three of them as they jumped into the car, shaking raindrops off of themselves as they did. After they were inside, Momar went around to the driver's seat and took his place behind the wheel.

There was a knock at the window next to Mara, and she lowered it a bit. A bearish, bearded face peered inside the vehicle. The skulls painted on his black helmet grinning in permanent rictus, orange flames flowing out of their empty eye sockets. "Welcome back to the outside, little girl." He smiled, showing a gold tooth.

Mara smiled back at him, "Thanks Mick. You take care of her for me?" She imagined the wind on her face even as she said the words.

"You know it. Come get her anytime." Mick shook the rain from his beard, and Momar cleared his throat once. "Uh, yeah. Got it. Time to go." Mara raised the window and tried to mentally prepare herself for the eventual grilling combined with a thorough visual inspection. It might wait until they were alone, but it would happen.

Momar had always been very thorough.

THREE

S o ... do you always travel like this?" Ethan asked. He touched the buttons on the door and the interior wood paneling with gentle swipes of his fingertips, as if the car were made of butterflies.

Mara nodded her head briefly. "Pretty much, yeah." She leaned forward and plugged her phone into the back of the middle seat console to charge it. Momar continued to send her laser eyes in the rearview mirror. She didn't need to look up to see his gaze—she could feel it as it traveled over her face.

"And really, thanks for the ride. I appreciate it." Ethan said. "Sir?" He spoke to Momar in the front seat. "Can you drop me at the Burnside Skatepark, please?" He gave a sheepish grin while he said it. Mara arched one eyebrow at his obvious sucking-up.

Max stared over at Ethan for a second, then said, "You rob a bank or something, dude?" Max's blond hair was rumpled and uneven, his face clean but looking like it had been freshly scrubbed against his will. Mara realized she was holding his slightly grubby hand in hers, and the feeling was like a hug.

My people. My baby brother. It's been so long.

Ethan laughed a little bit, obviously uncomfortable. "Uhh, no.

Nothing like that, little dude. I'm a good guy, honest. Yep. I'm good. All good." He looked from Max to Momar's back a couple of times, his face flushed.

After peering over at Ethan for a few tense seconds, Max responded with a shrug, "Okay. If my sister likes you, I like you." He then snuggled into Mara's side even closer, if that were possible.

The trip downtown was quick and quiet. Max, for once, was silent and seemed content to hold her hand. She let him. Mara could think of nothing better than to be with Max. And while Ethan was trying very hard to not act like a serial killer in front of her family, he only managed to look totally shifty in his long black duster over a black hoodie. Kinda hard to be all squeaky clean when you've just been sprung from juvenile detention. Still cute, though.

"You can pull in just up there, sir." Ethan pointed to a turnout next to the bridge, relief in his voice.

Momar guided the car into the place Ethan had showed him. Once the car was stopped, he turned and said, "I hope you have better luck in the future, young man. Stay safe." He bowed his head a bit toward Ethan.

"Thanks again for the ride," Ethan said to Momar. Then he turned to Mara, "And we'll talk soon, yes?" Mara nodded, a little smile curving up the corners of her mouth. He'd been a good friend on the inside. She really hoped he'd call or text her—he had definite possibilities and she didn't have many friends. Anywhere.

Ethan exited the car, then closed the door behind him. As they drove away, Mara could see him raising his hand in a goodbye wave. She would miss seeing him in group twice a week. It was the only thing in there she hadn't hated with a white-hot burning passion.

Without Ethan in the mix, the mood changed as soon as the car pulled away from the bridge. Max immediately dropped her hand and started talking a mile a minute. "I've really missed you, Mara. Things are weird when you're not at home. School was yucky. Oh, and you're not gonna believe it, I've got a surprise for you, too!" He leaned forward a little, looking up at her with so much happiness.

Mara patted his leg and smiled. "Hang on, buddy. Wait a sec ..." She turned her attention to Momar. Might as well get things out in the open sooner rather than later. "So what's with the escort? Am I all that dangerous now that I'm a hardened criminal?" She looked back at Max and winked.

Momar kept his attention on the road and said over his shoulder, "Much has changed since we last spoke." His voice sounded serious, but maybe ... maybe ...

For the first time in a long while, a small bit of hope crept into her. "You've got word about Mom and Dad? Are they okay? Do you know where they are?" They'd been missing as long as she'd been in Cascadia. While she'd never been all that close to either of her parents, she still worried. It wasn't like them to disappear for a year. Three months, maybe—if the scientific advancement was something they both were focused on and felt was worth spending their time and considerable wealth to explore. Sure, they were easily distracted by a new theory—how they'd found time to make two kids was a mystery. A gross mystery she absolutely didn't want to think about. But a year?

Momar's shoulders hunched up a tiny bit, and he shook his head. "There has been no news about your parents. I am sorry."

The hope crashed back into the nothingness Mara had felt for the last few months. She shook it off a little—after all, Max was here. She had him, and more importantly, she had to protect him and be a good big sister. They weren't any worse off with the 'rents still at large somewhere.

Momar continued after clearing his throat, "We will speak at home." Which was international code for "let's talk about the unpleasant stuff when the younger child is distracted or not around." Mara pursed her lips a little and nodded.

She let a sigh escape her, then patted Max's leg again and let her hand stay there for a minute, the warmth of him passing through his jeans into her hand. Her head leaned against the leather headrest, and her muscles relaxed in a way they hadn't in the past eleven months, two weeks and three days in lock-up. Max continued to chatter about nothing and everything he'd done while she'd been gone—school, friends, bugs, roadkill—all the things dearest to a young boy's heart. Mara commented from time to time, agreeing when she should and nodding her head at the appropriate times. But her thoughts couldn't help but keep circling around to Momar's proclamation. From the sound of things, the news wasn't good, although she'd think about that problem later. She was safe. She was with her family. Her brother.

Her people.

FOUR

Elona couldn't believe the day she was having. There she'd been, peacefully disassembling, cleaning, and lubing her 9mm in the Tower Armory when her stupid informant called on her stupid cell phone. He told her the idiot Layil girl had been released, apparently earlier in the day. Maybe even with enough time to make it to the safety of the family enclave. And the informant called her about it *now*.

She reattached the slide on the gun, function-tested it and then loaded it, damning her informant to hell and beyond for putting her in a very dangerous position.

This information would not go down well.

Shit. Shit. Shit. Elona placed the gun in her chest holster and her cell phone in the pocket of her suit jacket, then started walking down the hallway to where she knew a world of hurt awaited her. There was no way this would be forgotten or ignored. Her informant had failed her, which meant she had failed.

The girl was out.

Shit. Shit. Shit.

Elona left the Armory and walked toward the elevator that would take her to a very unpleasant meeting with her boss. The hall seemed to be endless, the only sound her heels clicking on the cement floor and the beating of her heart inside her ears. Halfway down the hallway, the overhead lights began to flicker and then dim.

This was not normal.

Elona stopped, the small hairs rising on her arms. Something was wrong. The lights flickered and dimmed again.

"Ssssinioch wants to sssseeeee you." A harsh, sibilant voice hissed out of the shadow of the corridor.

Fueled by pure adrenaline and years of training, Elona pulled her gun and fired a shot into the darkness, the bullet pinging off a pillar. In the flash of a second, she had seen the figure who had spoken to her. Adjusting her aim, she prepared to fire again when her hand snapped back toward her body. Elona screamed in pain as the gun dropped to the ground, her wrist held at an unnatural angle to her arm.

"Who'ssss a naughty girl, then?" The whispering taunted her.

Elona felt her body lurch forward, out of her control, one side moving forward and then the other as if she were a puppet on strings. "Let...me...go, Puppeteer." Her eyes bugged out of her head as she tried to get a better look at the hag controlling her. She'd expected pain and retribution, but this was a different kind of punishment.

"Ssssinioch wants to sssseeee you…" The bent and wrinkled figure chanted with each involuntary movement of Elona's body toward the doorway at the end of the corridor.

Elona had known it would be bad, with her failure rubbed in her face. She'd thought she might be forgiven if she blamed someone else down the food chain.

She was incorrect.

Shit. Shit. Shit.

FIVE

The Layil child's early release was, shall we say, unexpected?" Aeda said as she walked down the marble hall next to Sinioch. She straightened the edge of her figure-hugging tailored skirt and brushed an invisible wrinkle from her immaculate silk blouse, though she knew she looked perfect. She glanced sidelong at her husband, wondering what he might do to Elona. Aeda didn't hate the woman, and she certainly didn't want fewer Offspring in the world.

Sinioch ignored her glance and her conciliatory tone, and replied, "'Unexpected' changes nothing. Send Tenoch and his men for the Layil girl." While his anger could be fierce, his laser focus on their end goal was intoxicating.

She glanced at him as they approached the end of the hallway. Sinioch's suit was bespoke and fit him better than it should. His carriage and stride were that of a much younger man, and his power ... well, Aeda got a shiver thinking of the power. Combined, it was a heady mixture. It was almost a shame two First Borns were prohibited from having children together. While Aeda couldn't stand the little beasts, a child born of their collective powers would have made a formidable ally.

Aeda placated Sinioch by agreeing with him, since it mattered little to her. "A wise choice. She's only protected by the Scribe, Momar Singh." And with that, she wrote Elona off her mental list of underlings. The two of them entered the elevator and pressed the lower red button, which quickly transported them to the twenty-fourth floor of the Tower.

When they exited, she saw two very large men in black suits standing in front of the double door opposite the elevator. As Aeda and Sinioch approached, the guards lowered their heads in deference, precisely as they should.

Everyone needed to know their place in the world.

Aeda placed her hand on the palm-print reader on the right side and was scanned in a second. The door opened for them, the guards affecting a deeper bow as the two of them passed. Bowing in her presence pleased her.

Inside the lab, Aeda had to make an effort to stop her nose from wrinkling. The walls were covered with shelves and cupboards, beakers of who-knows-what on every surface. Sinioch never minded the bodily fluids and the smells and the clutter, though how she couldn't comprehend. While she believed in her husband and the causes he championed, his methods were sometimes rather messy. "She should be around the other side."

The two of them continued around a bank of file cabinets to another part of the lab. Aeda saw Elona cowering against a wall, with one arm held above her head, the hand bloody and broken.

It really was unfortunate she'd disappointed Sinioch. Elona just didn't look her normal put-together self when she was having the life beaten out of her.

Elona saw them and started spouting nonsense, "The Layil girl wasn't supposed to ..."

At that moment, Elona's arm snapped backward at the elbow and she screamed. Aeda looked left and right to see where the Puppeteer was hiding. "That's enough. Show yourself, wraith." She might be a means to an end, but Aeda didn't have to like the freakish hag.

A mostly human figure slid out of the shadows, lanky white hair falling around a face like a desiccated tomato. Aeda grimaced with distaste.

At her side, Sinioch said, "You've had your fun, haven't you?" The Puppeteer gave a small bow to him, losing focus on her victim momentarily.

Elona took advantage of her freedom and made a move toward Sinioch, her pain evident in every movement. "Please, I swear it wasn't ... I mean, I didn't know. My man at the prison never said a—"

Sinioch pulled a dagger from the inside pocket of his jacket, which stopped Elona immediately. Aeda could see the telltale bumps on Elona's shoulder blades clearly through what was left of her shirt, but being an Offspring wouldn't help her anymore. Not with Sinioch anyway. It was a shame, really. Elona had had potential.

He said, "You have failed me, Elona. You know how important this is to me, which should be the only thing that matters to you. Now you have a choice. Death or ..." He held out the dagger. Aeda blinked a couple of times. Her mate was offering Elona a way out. After all their years together, he could still surprise her.

Elona gasped. "It's forbidden. You can't kill me. I'm Offspring." Aeda rolled her eyes. Maybe Elona hadn't as much potential after all if she couldn't see what he clearly meant. He'd given her a chance at a merciful end, and all she could do was spout idiotic ancient law.

Sinioch raised one eyebrow. "Ah, yes, the rules of the Covenant. How convenient." He nodded toward the silent Puppeteer, who instantly raised her hands. Elona stood against her will as the Puppeteer forced her to shuffle toward Sinioch. About three feet away from him, Elona's unbroken hand extended out, shaking with effort and fear.

He laid the dagger in her hand. "Again, you have a choice, my dear." This time he spoke to her like she was mentally addled. He nodded to the Puppeteer once more, and she dropped her hands. Elona was free again, with a knife and a decision to make. "And you choose ...?"

Elona stared at the blade in her hand, then at Sinioch and Aeda. The penny finally dropped, and she understood her options. She slowly raised the blade to her throat, hand trembling, tears rolling down her cheeks. A second later, she dropped the blade with a clatter and stared down at it on the floor.

Sinioch shook his head and sighed. "Very well."

Aeda shrugged her shoulders. He'd been as kind as he could, giving Elona a clean exit. And still she'd chosen the other path. Pity. But at least she'd give them more data in the study of the drugs. Aeda pushed a button on the wall nearest her. A panel slid open, displaying three large steel tables with restraints built into them. One table was occupied by what looked like a large man, or what used to be a man. He wore nothing except a pair of grayish underwear, his arm strapped down, and an IV with blue liquid dripping into him. The odious scientist peon stood next to the man making notes on a clipboard. When the peon saw Sinioch, Aeda and Elona, he grinned, his eyes getting a dewy and dreamy look to them. Again, Aeda grimaced. He may have gotten results, but he really was the most horrid creature.

Elona's response to seeing the tableau was immediate. She tried to make a grab for the knife on the ground, but Sinioch stepped on it before she could get there. "Unfortunately, you've already made your choice, my dear." He nodded at the Puppeteer again, who forced Elona to walk to one of the empty steel tables, her screams echoing as the panel closed behind her.

Aeda let out a small sigh—a verbal check mark on a to-do list. Elona had been dealt with and was now forgotten. Offspring were valuable, but not the ones who failed at their jobs. Aeda's mind had already moved on to prioritize the other tasks at hand she needed to complete. Their end goal was for the betterment of their kind, and to gain their rightful place in the world. This sacred vision, the vision Sinioch and Aeda had birthed and shared and nurtured, would not come to pass without diligence and hard work.

They were nothing if not diligent.

Six

If seeing the actual outside world hadn't been such an unexpected thrill, the warmth of the car and the gentle hum of the motor would have kept Mara's head leaned back and pushed her straight into sleepy time. But the traffic, clouds, and even the rain couldn't dampen the excitement of not being locked up anymore. She pressed her face against the window to see everything she had missed—the bridges over the river, green hills, the tall buildings of the downtown cityscape, and, finally, the driveway to the Layil family home.

"Driveway" was probably underselling it. The family abode was, in fact, a very large mansion, with its own road and wrought iron gate. The trees on each side of the road, along with an edging of manicured grass, made it seem like they had entered a completely private green tunnel.

After the gate opened and the caravan passed through, Mara could see the multistoried main house looking exactly as it had her whole life. The Range Rover continued down the drive until it came to a stop in front of the steps leading up to the double door entry.

"Come on ..." Max had unbuckled and opened the door and was

already tugging on her hand to lead her inside. Mara couldn't keep the smile from her face as she followed Max's lead. At least the rain had stopped for now, so she could take her time breathing in the freedom.

At the top of the brick steps, a small coffee-skinned woman in an orange and red sari waited for Mara, her hands clasped in front of her and a worried smile on her face. Her bindi jewel sparkled in the light as she made a small bow. Mara and Max walked up to her, and Mara held out her arms. Best scones on the planet came from those floury fingertips, she thought.

"We have all missed you," said Dadima, hugging her. When she let Mara go, she held her at arms-length and looked her up and down, like some kind of scanner. Mara spun around once so Dadima could inspect every side. *Some people bugged the crap outta you, and some people could do the exact same thing and it was okay. Better than okay. It was right.*

"I've missed you, too." Mara said, and then gave Dadima a quick kiss on the cheek to show her how much. Dadima hid her smile behind a hand and waved Mara off.

"Come on—let's go, slowpoke." Max tugged on her hand again, leading her inside. The foyer had always intimidated Mara, so much marble, oak, and polished brass. It looked like a very posh hotel lobby—a hotel that had always made her feel like an outsider, unworthy and uncomfortable. Her most prominent childhood memory was of being escorted out of the main rooms of the house, including the foyer, and into the nursery playroom.

The little dude kept up the pressure on her arm. "Mara—are you listening?" Dadima smiled at both Layils and followed them into the house, with Momar closing the doors behind them.

Once inside, Max said again, "Come ON." He continued to pull on her hand, trying to lead her somewhere only important to eleven-year-old boys. Mara slowed her walking a little bit. It wasn't often she'd appreciated being home, and it felt like maybe she'd be missing an opportunity if she didn't do it now. Since everything was an emergency to Max, he could wait a few more seconds.

Momar patted Mara's shoulder and said, "Welcome home, Memsahib," before giving a small bow. His tall slim frame looked elegant in his suit, his *gatka* training keeping him young and strong for someone older than dirt. And for Momar—her guardian and trainer—that hint of emotion was like a bear hug, flowers, and skywriting all combined into one.

Mara stopped, even though Max still had a death grip on her arm. "Now, can you tell me why Mick and Jackie were with us?" She had a feeling her brother wouldn't hear the question if she said it in a regular bored voice. She was right. Max had completely ignored her comment while still trying to wrangle her somewhere.

"It is time we spoke alone." Momar nodded to Max as if Mara could teleport him away. Like the little dude was ever going to let go of her.

Max kept the pressure on, using all his body weight to pull on her hand. He had as much success as a dachshund trying to move an elephant.

"Mara, can we go now? Come on, I want to show you—"

"It will be a pleasure to have a serious *gatka* student again, since my current student—" Momar interrupted the boy, then raised one eyebrow at Max "—lacks patience, shall we say?"

That got Max's attention, finally. "Hey, I'm not that bad ..." He dropped Mara's hand and did a spin-kick toward Momar, who simply stepped backward to avoid Max's foot. Momar and Mara chuckled, and even Max got a goofy grin on his face. "It's kinda fun, but I get sweaty."

With the smile lingering on his face, Momar swiveled his focus back to Mara. "Really, though, we must talk." The smile didn't linger very long. He nodded toward the right, which could have meant any of three or four rooms on the main floor.

Mara got the message. "Yeah, I know. Things have changed. Dark tidings and all that. But I'm kinda damp and wearing year-old clothes. Can I have a minute to change? Both of you?" She looked from Max to Momar. Surely they'd understand and give her a freaking break.

At least Momar sighed and nodded before adding, "I'll be in the study." Whew. One down.

Mara didn't wait for her brother's permission but headed to her room up the wide staircase. Max followed behind her like a puppy. She turned and said, "Did you hear that, Max? He called me Memsahib? He only ever called Mom that." Not necessarily a good thing, but at least it was a conversation starter. Not like they'd ever needed something to get them talking, or to get Max talking.

Usually it took a bug, or a cool car, or a tree, or air ...

"Yeah. Okay, sure. Fine." He sighed at being blown off. "Anyway, I made you a surprise, and ..." Max started to wind up again, his enthusiasm not dampened a bit by rain or adult stuff.

"Seriously, little man, I just need a few minutes. Okay?" She stopped on the landing and turned to him.

"It's at the fort, see, and—" His face beamed excitement, and he practically danced from foot to foot.

Mara shook her head and stopped him with a held-up finger. "No way, dude. I am not going back out into the rain right now ..." Max's face fell, her words taking all the wind from his sails.

He said, looking at the carpet, "Okay. I get it." His shoulders collapsed a little, like he'd had his bones removed. The eager puppy had been replaced by a beaten dog.

Mara felt a wave of guilt wash over her. He'd been just as much in solitary as she had, only in a big house with servants. A whole year with only Momar and Dadima to talk to outside of school. She put her hands on his shoulders and knelt to his level. "Oh, buddy, I'm sorry."

Max sniffed once, still avoided eye contact. "No. Fine. I can wait." He sniffed again. With feeling. He'd played her emotions like a brand-new video game.

He couldn't see her face, so she let the smile break out. The little actor almost got her with his award-winning performance—she knew she shouldn't give in, but dang it, the kid was good. "Okay, what the heck—I'm already damp. Let's go see whatever it is you want me to see." She stood back up and watched his miraculous recovery.

Max's face beamed again, and he almost jumped up with excitement. "Really? You mean it?" Wow, had she called that one correctly.

Now she did laugh, "Really. But we don't want Momar's turban in a wad, so let's take—"

Max finished for her, "The back stairs!" He grabbed her hand and pulled her the rest of the way, both of them laughing as they went.

SEVEN

The two motorcycle-riding bodyguards sat on the front steps of the Layil mansion smoking cigars as if they were celebrating something. *Foolish. Very, very foolish.* Tenoch adjusted the binoculars one click, his breathing even and steady. Patience was the key. Was always the key. He had not risen to be Sinioch's chief tracker by accident.

A small movement caught his peripheral vision on one side, and he saw the bright blond heads of the Layil children as they darted across the perfect green lawn and into the dense forest that ringed the estate. With one hand, he kept the binoculars trained on them, and with the other, he pushed a button on the thick metal band around his wrist.

"Tala, Kobi—they are in the woods heading down the hill. You know what to do." Tenoch's heart beat a little faster with the anticipation of both the hunt and the catch. They were so close.

"Intercept."

Eight

The fort was exactly the way she'd left it a few years ago, although the forest seemed both smaller and bigger than she remembered. The trees dampened sounds, and even Max's plaintive "Come ON!" every fifteen seconds seemed quieter and less irritating. Mara couldn't believe anything made of wood had survived in the pervasive damp and shade, but maybe moss was a preservative. Sheets of plywood nailed to wooden pallets formed the walls, and corrugated tin made up the roof. She'd made windows with the pallets too, though they were really just holes in the walls. In the shadow of the giant fir trees, the structure seemed to be part of the forest floor more than anything man-made.

"You are SO slow, Mara ..." Max said, his hand on the doorway of the fort. Not much fit inside the one room, basically two people and a couple of rickety chairs, but it had been her escape pod and she loved it. "Okay, wait there," he said as she stood in the entrance.

Max had his hand on an old gray tarp that covered something. His big reveal, probably. It might be a skull or a skeleton, knowing Max and his gathering tendencies. There was nothing too gross for him.

"All right. I'm here. Where's the fire, little man?" Mara hoped she wouldn't have to vomit after seeing his surprise and cringed a little bit.

"Ta-da!" Max pulled the tarp off, revealing a hand-carved wooden piece. It sat on an old table, an elongated oval of Douglas fir wood, with two rows of six small depressions, and one larger depression on each end. There were small stones and acorns scattered in the holes, just waiting for something to happen. The wood surface looked smooth and sanded, but natural. No stain or paint.

Mara's jaw dropped. She looked at Max, who glowed with pride and wiggled his eyebrows up and down, just like her father. "You made this?" She blurted out.

"Yep. Mancala board. All by myself. Momar doesn't know about the pocketknife Dad gave me." He patted the board. "And Mick gave me sandpaper so we wouldn't get slivers."

"This is—it's fantastic! You did an amazing job, although we'll talk about knife skills later, okay? I absolutely love it!" Mara reached over to him and pulled him into a hug. "You know, though, I'm still not gonna let you win, because that teaches you nothing. You'll have to beat me fair and square."

He grinned up at her. "Like I need to learn Mancala? I'm gonna crush you." He pushed away from her and pulled one of the chairs up to the table, sitting below one of the empty window frames letting light inside.

Mara realized her clothes had only gotten wetter after the tramp through the forest, and she wiggled back and forth a little. The year-old tights seem to have wicked dampness into spots she knew hadn't been in contact with the vegetation. "Hey, can we play later, dude? Momar's gonna kick my—"

Two muscular arms clad in black reached through the window and pulled Max out of the fort in one swift movement. Mara was frozen for a microsecond, not comprehending what she'd seen.

As she regained her senses, she screamed her brother's name and lunged toward the window, but something stopped her. She looked down to see gloved hands grasping her middle and quickly spun around to break their hold. When she turned, she saw what she was up against, a very large man dressed like some kind of army-ninja-killing machine. She tried a spin-kick on him, but there wasn't enough room in the fort and he easily waved it away. It'd been too long since she practiced. He backed her into a corner and made a quick grab for her, one arm wrapping around her, one hand clamping down on her mouth to keep her quiet.

He carried her out of the fort, Mara kicking and struggling with every step. She screamed against his palm, but it made no difference. Outside, she saw another man standing quietly, with binoculars in his hand and some kind of silver metal rod-thing hanging from his belt. He was built like a tank and dressed all in black like the other ninja assholes. He said, "Quickly, Kobi. Car."

"Yes, Tenoch," the man holding her responded.

Tenoch and Kobi. *Remember their names.*

She took a breath and focused on everything Momar had taught her, bucking her body back and forth. The man who held her, Kobi apparently, tried to adjust his grip, and as he did, Mara gave all her energy to one kick back into his groin. He dropped her like a rock, Mara landing on her side. She felt the air leave her lungs in a whoosh, unable to catch another breath.

The guy in charge, Tenoch, said, "I see you live up to your billing." His voice was bored, and he pulled the metal wand from his side, pushing a button. A blue crackle of electricity sparked at the end.

Mara's surprise and fear turned to rage boiling up from her center.

These. Assholes. Took. Max.

She managed to sit up and get one partial breath inside before she screamed, "NO!"

With her scream, she felt a wave of energy burst out of her like a shock grenade. Tenoch and Kobi were blown back and away from her. The Kobi guy was thrust into the fort, wood splintering. Tenoch went backward into a tree trunk, his electric wand spinning away as his body came into contact with the cold, hard bark.

Mara looked around in confusion, unsure what had just happened. After a second or two, she realized she needed to take advantage of the assholes being down. She ran over to Tenoch and picked up the shock wand next to him. Tenoch looked up at her, gasping, his breath knocked out of him. "You bastard," she said.

She pushed the same button she'd seen him use and poked the wand into his ribcage, hard. The zap seemed to do the trick, even on someone as big and bad looking as this Tenoch dude.

Kobi was inside what was left of the fort, a nasty wound in his side from a piece of a board stuck in him. He groaned but wasn't really conscious. Mara pushed the button on the wand again but couldn't bring herself to shock him. He was already in pretty bad shape. She threw the wand as far as she could into the woods, not wanting to touch anything belonging to the bastards who'd kidnapped her brother.

Max.

Where was the asshole who'd grabbed Max? She ran around to the side where he'd been snatched through the window, but there was no one there, and no trail to follow. Just trees and undergrowth. Her heart wrenched and she swallowed hard a couple of times. It had already been a couple of minutes since those horrible arms had reached through the window.

They could be anywhere.

She needed help. She needed Momar.

NINE

*R*un. *Get Momar. Max needs you.*

Mara sprinted through the forest. Her boots slipped here and there, and she didn't even notice she was screaming Momar's name over and over. The wet undergrowth wrapped around her as she ran, her clothes getting wetter and heavier with every step.

Run. Get Momar. Max ...

Finally through the woods, she found a little more energy to race over the grass to the house, still yelling at the top of her lungs. As she approached the back patio, she saw Mick and Jackie scrambling around from the front of the house and coming toward her.

"What the hell is going on?" Mick bellowed. He grabbed her by her shoulders, stopping her.

Mara yelled back at him, "Momar! I need Momar!" She panted with effort, then shook him off and took the steps two at a time, adrenaline pushing her forward.

She burst into the kitchen, her muddy boots leaving skid marks as she practically bowled into Momar, who was already hurrying in her direction.

"What happened?" he asked, grasping her arms, his face lined with concern. He must have heard her screams.

Mara gasped, "They took Max, they took Max ..." She could hardly catch a breath and her heart hammered in her chest.

Momar said, "Who took him? Who was it?" He gripped her arms harder, his eyes boring into hers, intent on seeing everything.

"No, we have to go back out to the fort, we have to go ..." Mara struggled to get free, but his hands were like iron. "They took him, they took him ..." She babbled.

Momar's fingers pinched into her, hard. "Stop. Focus. What happened?" He almost willed concentration into her through his hands.

She felt a small island of calm and tried to focus on it. She took one deep breath in. "We snuck out to the fort. Max surprised me with a Mancala game, and then there were big, scary men and they grabbed him ... and then me ... I tried to stop them ... I tried to help ..." Mara felt rage and fear, so much fear.

Momar spun his head around and nodded at Mick and Jackie, who had followed them into the kitchen. They ran out the door as fast as they were able. Momar's hands still grasped Mara's shoulders.

"Let me go—I want to help." She struggled to get free of him, but Momar was far stronger and not winded from a run back to the house. He pulled her toward a chair and pushed her down into it.

"We cannot lose you as well. It is too dangerous." He shook his head sadly.

"Who are they? Why did they take Max?" Mara had so many questions. "Momar," she said, a catch in her voice, "please tell me what's going on." Tears welled up in her eyes. The morning had been a dream—being reunited with her brother, being home. And now, everything was turned upside down again. There was a bitter taste in her mouth.

He looked at her, his brown eyes looking the way she felt—sad, angry, and afraid. "We will find Max. This, I swear."

TEN

I ... I hurt them. It was me." Mara looked at her own upturned palms, then turned them over to look at the back of her hands, too. How had those huge men ended up bleeding and unconscious? What had she done? Had she done anything, or had she imagined it all?

"Tell me what happened," Momar said. His voice tried hard to be even and tranquil, but Mara wasn't ready to go there yet. There was too much to process.

"It's like I blew them up. I was so angry—" She was interrupted by the slam of a door, so loud it made her jump a little.

Mick and Jackie were back, but they didn't have Max. Just news of what they found in the woods.

"It was like some kinda bomb went off in the place, everything was in pieces," Mick said, his breath catching in his throat a bit.

Jackie was also panting, but managed to say, "And there was one piece of wood covered in ... blood." Mara felt her knees go numb at the description of the fort. And blood? What happened had been real if Jackie had seen it, too. *Oh, Max ...*

Mick continued, "We looked but they're gone. Somebody did some major damage."

Jackie dropped a long skinny piece of metal on the counter. "And we found this."

Momar picked up the wand and inspected it closely. "Miyamoto Industries." He took a deep breath and turned to Mick. "We must go to the monastery. Immediately. It's no longer safe here."

"Monastery?" Mara and Jackie said at the same time. They turned to each other, without a shred of humor on either side. Who needed monks when there's been a kidnapping?

Mick said, "Long story, Jackie. Tell you later."

Mara's pulse continued to increase, and she felt her face flush. "Tell *her* later? Really? And why haven't we called the police already?!? Seriously, we need to call the police! Now!" She had made a fist and slammed it on the table.

Momar covered her hand with his, and Mara threw it off. "This is not police business," he said with a sigh. "It is my sworn duty to protect you. Trust me and soon everything will be made clear." He turned to Jackie. "Please take her upstairs and help her get ready. We leave in 10 minutes."

Jackie nodded and made a lifting motion with her hands in front of Mara.

Fuming, isolated, and full of questions, Mara stood up to do as she'd been told. For now.

ELEVEN

Back in the Range Rover in what felt like seconds, Mara touched the outline of her phone in her right pocket—the only thing she'd been able to smuggle out under Jackie's eagle eye. A change of clothes after her shower? Sure. But no pictures, no clothes—she'd not been allowed to take anything.

Momar drove the car, easily negotiating the rainy, twisty road. Mara sat in the passenger seat next to him, giving him the side-eye to make sure his attention was focused anywhere but on her. Her anger hadn't dissipated one tiny bit, and none of her questions or concerns had been addressed.

She was done with relying on the adults around her.

Pretending to look out the window, she glanced down at her phone and saw 148 New Messages flashing over the top. With two clicks, she hit Delete All. After another side-glance, she moved her thumb to dial, then hit Call.

Through the speaker system of the car, a voice said, "9-1-1. What's your emergency?"

Before Mara could say a single syllable, Momar reached out and hit the hang up button on the dashboard. He sighed once.

"Memsahib, please. You must trust me. Police cannot help."

"You are a complete—" Before Mara could get any of the names out she wanted to call him, the speaker system rang again.

"I believe this involves the disappearance of your parents," he said just loud enough to be heard over the ringing sound. "If your questions are not answered at the monastery, I will not stop you from calling the police." Another ring. "But you will not call them now."

Shit. Mara looked at him with murder in her eyes, but she hit Answer Call.

"Hello?" she chirped in her best fake-happy voice.

"This number dialed 9-1-1. Is there an emergency?" The operator sounded deadly serious. Mara opened her mouth to reply and nothing came out. She looked over at Momar, who wore a grimace and shook his head. "Hello? Is anyone there?"

It felt like an eternity before she made up her mind. "I'm so sorry, my little brother ..." she swallowed a bit, "uh, my little brother was playing with my phone and accidentally dialed. Really sorry about that." The lie flowed out of her like water, but she continued to shoot mental daggers at Momar.

"We keep record of these kinds of calls. If it happens again, we'll send a car to check on you. Do you understand?"

Mara fake smiled even though the dispatcher couldn't see her and imagined going back to juvie because of a stupid phone issue. She shuddered. "I understand. So sorry."

The phone clicked off, and Momar hit End Call to be sure. She heard him inhale deeply.

Mara slumped in her seat. "I hate Bluetooth."

TWELVE

The monastery was in a manor house almost as large as the Layil estate, but the gates seemed more imposing and less homey, if that was even a thing. Mara would have been more interested in looking at all the details if she didn't keep hearing Max's scream in her head, immediately followed by Momar's "Trust me."

Trust. He'd been the first person she thought of after Max was taken, the adult she thought would get something accomplished. Momar had been a constant presence in her life, the one person she'd relied on even when they disagreed. But now that she considered it, where had he been when she got sentenced? Where had he been for her parents? And now Max?

Mara's stomach had tied itself into knots, while her exterior felt pulled in all directions at once. *I'm human taffy.*

She looked around, realizing the car had driven through the gates and stopped in front of the steps to the house. While Mick and Jackie parked their bikes behind the Rover, Momar had already exited the car. Mara exhaled one breath and stayed buckled into her seat. *Make him wait.*

Mick appeared at the passenger door, opening it and nodding at her once. She remained seated, her arms crossed on her chest.

Momar walked around the Range Rover vehicle and stood next to Mick, both staring at her. Momar said to Mick out of one side of his mouth, "I will call you soon. You and Jackie may go now." More adult nonsense she would be kept out of, no doubt. The two men continued to look at her, their expressions calm.

Her temper flared again, and Mara undid her seat belt then leaped out of the car. She heard the door shut behind her but didn't look back at either Mick or Momar. She stood there, not knowing where to go, although she would guess the large front door would be an adequate start. As she made the move toward it, Momar glided in front of her, leading her in that direction as if it had been planned the whole time.

The door was answered by a small Japanese girl, who bowed once to Momar and backed away to let the two of them inside. She led them through what looked like a museum of dark wood and library furniture. After about ten steps, Mara couldn't control herself any longer.

"Stop. Just stop." She said, doing just that.

The girl and Momar followed suit.

"How are a bunch of monks going to help Max?" She was done with the insanity and turned to go back the way she'd come in, her fists balled at her sides.

The girl looked at Mara's face closely, then placed a hand on her shoulder. "Your lip is bleeding." With her other hand she reached out and touched Mara's split lip with one featherlight finger, her head cocked to one side ever so slightly.

Mara didn't have a chance to react but batted the girl's hand away a split second late. "What the actual hell do you think you're doing?"

The girl smiled from ear to ear. "See? All better." She nodded at Mara.

Mara licked her lip with her tongue and found the split was gone, her lip smooth, and the blood vanished. Her mouth dropped open a little bit, her head cocked to one side. *Wait, what?* Her anger temporarily evaporated, replaced once again by confusion.

The girl smiled. "I'm Hiroko. You got the shoulder bumps too?" She spun sideways so Mara could see her shoulder blades, and then hunched forward to tighten her shirt, the bumps becoming visible. She turned back and linked her arm in Mara's. "Makes swimsuits a bitch, huh?"

Mara nodded once, her head trying to make sense of everything. *There are others like me?*

Momar smiled a little, as much as he ever did. "Hiroko's family is like yours, Mara."

Hiroko chimed in, "Well, we're not as cool—I mean, we don't have a Scribe or anything." She smiled again at Mara, indicating with her eyes she was talking about Momar.

"Scribe?" There were words being used she knew, but what they were saying was completely foreign. Mara saw two black-robed monks approach them and bow slightly as they walked past.

"Yes, Memsahib, I am a Scribe," Momar said patiently, as if to a toddler.

"And only the most important families still have one, you know." Hiroko giggled like a star-struck teenager. Momar raised an eyebrow at her. "Sorry. I'll be quiet now."

Mara followed, her mouth slightly open, her eyes darting from side to side. What world had she entered? What world considered her weirdo oddball family a most important one? What the hell was happening?

They passed a dark alcove in the hallway, where an ebony-skinned young woman sat in a classic Lotus pose, surrounded by candles and incense. Her eyes closed, she looked like anyone who meditated, except she floated about eight inches off the ground.

Mara craned her neck to look closer at the woman, but they kept moving. "Did you see ...?"

Momar ignored the levitating woman and Mara's comment. "My family has served your father's line for more than 500 years. We protect, train, and record."

She forgot floating people. "Five hundred—that's crazy. I thought you were like a butler or an assistant to my dad." Mara focused on a word. "Served? Your family is some kind of slave to mine?" An infantile part of her, still fuming mad at Momar, kind of wished he'd damn well do what she asked.

Momar shook his head. "No. We *freely* serve the Layil line because your family is powerful, and fights *for* the Covenant."

"Fights for the what? And what does it have to do with Max?"

Mara wondered if she was still in juvie and someone had coldcocked her with a cast-iron pan.

The group stopped in front of a set of large wooden doors. Hiroko spoke in mock-serious tones, her voice almost the singsong of parody. "You know, *the Covenant*. Rules that govern a parallel world that has existed on earth for millennia." At that point she actually laughed. Momar's eyes narrowed and shot laser beams at her.

Hiroko pursed her lips together to keep any more mirth from escaping and opened the doors.

Momar gestured for Mara to step inside. "It's time to learn what you are."

Thirteen

Light beamed through incense smoke in the long room. Mara saw rows of robed men sitting with their legs crossed in front of them, softly chanting in unison, and one really old man standing on the raised platform directly across from her at the far end. He held a wooden staff in one hand, maybe to prop himself up. He looked about three centuries past due for a beard trim.

There was a whisper in Mara's ear. "The abbot sees many things." Hiroko was serious this time. She moved to Mara's side, linked an arm in hers, and gently pulled her toward the platform. As they approached him, the elderly man descended the three stairs with the aid of his staff.

They arrived at the bottom step at the same time.

Hiroko dropped Mara's arm and bowed her head slightly. "Abbot Greb, this is Mara Layil."

The abbot handed his staff to Hiroko and reached his hands out toward Mara's face. Mara pulled back, not sure what was happening, but Hiroko patted her shoulder and gave her a little push forward.

His hands were light as a puff of wind across her cheeks and nose, tracing the outlines of her bones. A tiny smile curved the corner of his mouth. "You are your father's daughter."

She'd just been face-palmed by what appeared to be a blind monk. *Awesome.* The day just kept getting better. When would they help her find Max?

His fingers left her face as quickly as they had arrived, and Abbot Greb held his hand out for his staff, which Hiroko gave him. He turned and walked away from the girls, toward a normal-sized door in the wall.

Hiroko gave another gentle push and said, "He'll help you understand. I promise." She smiled at Mara, who looked back to Momar for confirmation. As always, he was three steps behind her, and he nodded, confirming she was to follow the abbot. She thought briefly about not doing it, just to spite them all, but her curiosity was piqued.

The doorway led to a small and modest room, with a table and chairs in the middle. The abbot stopped there and reached into a small box, withdrawing a few wooden matches. He struck one on the table and reached unerringly for the large pillar candle sitting in the center. He lit three candles without a single hesitation, and Mara shook her head, wondering if the face-thing was an act.

"Unlike my guests, I don't need light to see, but it seems the polite thing to do."

"So, uh, you're some kind of preacher?" Organized religion wasn't Mara's thing, nor was it her parents', but she needed a place to start. Apparently, small talk wasn't her thing, either.

He turned to face her. "I am a monk, child." He walked to a simple bookcase a few feet away.

"What's the difference?" It came out sounding like she was being a smart-ass, and she winced a little at her tone of voice. She may have been mad, but she wasn't mad at this guy.

The abbot pulled a large book from the case and turned back to her. "More similar than different, I suppose." He crossed back to the table, his steps slow and measured. "For centuries, my order has followed a secret charge, a sacred duty."

Mara noticed a Mancala game on the table, and her fingers moved a few of the seeds in the hollows.

Abbot Greb smiled. "Your father and I played together many times." He set the book on the table, rattling the seeds.

Mara looked up from the game, paying close attention to the face of the old monk. She cocked her head to one side a little. "You know my dad?"

The abbot nodded. "Yes, child. I know him well." Mara felt a small glimmer of hope when the old man used the present tense. He reached toward the book and opened it. The room filled with a golden light, the page in the book glowing. "Come around and see."

Mara started to shake her head before realizing two things; first, he couldn't see her, and second, Momar trusted this guy. Chirpy little Hiroko trusted this guy. And it sounded like her father had trusted this guy.

She did as he asked.

"May I have your hand?" he asked. She ignored.

"What is this?" Mara pointed to the book, then rolled her eyes because he still couldn't see her.

"Many answers you seek are here." He said, waving a hand over the shining pages. "Your father and his father before him were shown this. I hope you, too, find comfort in it."

Mara looked down and saw something a little disturbing. For the second time in a very short time span, she wondered if she was unconscious in the infirmary at the detention center.

"Free will guides all creation, from the eternal to the mortal." As he said the words, the book's script and drawings animated and began to move.

"That's not possible." She shook her head. *Oh yeah, I've been knocked out.*

"Listen, child." He touched the page gently, and a different image arose, a group of white, winged, human-shaped things in a large expanse of what looked like sky. "Once, outside the stream of mortal time, twelve eternal beings called Watchers sought to know mortality." He turned the page.

The next picture was of twelve winged creatures in a huge desert.

"They yearned to understand human love. Love not by virtue of creation, but freely given and freely accepted. So they asked the Creator for mortality and it was granted." He turned the page.

Now the picture showed the twelve beings, human, but trapped and staggering under the weight of massive wings.

"Every choice has a consequence. The Twelve became human,

but their once glorified wings manifested as cold, painful metal. No earthly ore was strong enough to sever their wings, so one of the Twelve offered herself as a sacrifice."

The next page showed a funeral pyre, flames licking the body of one of the beings.

"The sacrificed one's wings were melted and forged into a great sword. With that sword, each of the Eleven's wings were in turn cut from their bodies, melted, and forged into other relics."

The abbot turned the page once more. It was a family tree with many sections, the branches growing and unfurling as Mara watched.

"The remaining Eleven spread throughout the world and took human husbands and wives. They bore children, called First Born, each possessing incredible power." He turned from the book, his sightless eyes staring straight into Mara. "Your grandfather was one of the First Born, a name given to those sons and daughters of the Eleven."

Mara's hand reached up toward her shoulder, arching over it and toward her back and her odd shoulder bumps. She shook her head. "Look, this is Harry Potter stuff. There's no way I can believe—"

The abbot interrupted her. "Our kind have been called sorcerers, vampires, demons. Our world—your world—has existed mostly hidden away, but when glimpsed has always been feared and misunderstood."

She took a step backward, still shaking her head. The abbot reached out and grabbed her arm. "Let go of me—"

Mara twisted out of his grasp.

Abbot Greb held out his other hand. "My child, your brother is in grave danger, but we can help." He smiled a bit, a sad and world-weary smile. "Please. Trust an old monk."

She closed her eyes for a second, going over the checklist in her head of who could help her and Max. And her parents. Her family was who-knows-where, and in pretty serious danger, from what he'd implied. And Momar trusted this guy. Hiroko trusted this guy. Her dad had trusted this guy.

Mara opened her eyes and placed her hand in his.

The abbot nodded and looked at her again, his head turning to one side as if he was listening to something. He inhaled a bit. "You are Turning far too soon." The abbot's eyebrows scrunched together, like he was trying to make sense of something.

Enough was enough. He said he could help but he just wanted to spout nonsensical jibber jabber, not *do* anything. Mara tried to pull away, but the abbot tightened his grip.

"Hmmm, there is something more here." He squeezed her hand and she pulled away once, hard, finally breaking the old man's grip. "This cannot be ..." He shook his head, his face losing the benevolent old grandpa look.

Now he looked pissed. And a little scared. He reached out for his staff.

Mara backed away, edging toward the doorway to the prayer room. The door opened of its own accord and bounced back against the wall on the other side, creating a sound like a cannon shot. She spun around and saw Momar and Hiroko staring, eyes wide from the commotion.

"Hiroko, the Layil child must leave." Abbot Greb was right behind Mara but spoke directly to the other girl. His eyes swiveled to Momar. "What have you done?"

Mara's jaw hardened, her anger and frustration resurging through her body. "This place is a looney bin. I'm leaving." She directed the words to Momar but looked at the abbot and Hiroko too, then stomped away.

Behind her, she heard Momar's voice. "Hiroko, please stay with her while I speak to the abbot."

FOURTEEN

Momar watched the two girls walk out of the room, then bowed once to the abbot, and said, "Please. We need your help." He'd studied and trained and prepared for everything, or so he'd thought. But this—he'd never imagined someone would harm the children.

Abbot Greb turned his whitened eyes to face Momar. "If what I sensed in her is true—" he shook his head "—you have brought great danger to us all. I must speak to Armaros, but for now, I must ask you to leave and to take the child with you."

Before Momar could open his mouth to protest, the abbot spun and crossed back to the small room where he'd been with Mara.

The door slammed shut behind him.

FIFTEEN

Mara opened the driver's side door, reached under the seat of the Range Rover, and found the extra set of keys right where she'd been expecting them. Hiroko stood beside her, chattering away, and attempting to make her feel better.

She would have none of it. Her brother had been kidnapped and could be hurt or ... Mara felt her stomach clench at the other options. She couldn't think of anything but getting Max back in one piece.

"Look, no one wants to help me find Max. My options are limited. You can either be in or out." Mara faced Hiroko and lifted her hands up in a gesture of futility. "Your choice."

Hiroko looked at the monastery and the open doorway, then nodded her head. "Okay. I'm in."

"Then get in the car. We're leaving." Mara climbed into the driver's seat while Hiroko scampered around to the passenger side. "Buckle up."

The engine roared to life, or rather purred to life, and Mara put the car into gear.

As she pressed the gas pedal, she saw a movement on the imposing front porch—Momar had exited the building and was frantically waving at her.

Mara felt even more anger surge through her, and she stomped hard on the accelerator.

Scribe. Service. Families. Duty. Honor. None of the words meant more than Max.

Hiroko waved at Momar. "Bye!"

Sixteen

All Max could see was a bed with a small table next to it, and a stainless-steel toilet in the corner. The walls of the room were made of clear thick glass or plastic, but lights were shining on the front so he couldn't see out. He sat huddled on the floor, his arms clasped around his knees, which were drawn up to his chest. He shook a little bit, and he tried to wipe the tears off his face.

A loud thump on his left got his attention. He realized he could see into another cell like his next to him. And in that cell was a large man wearing only some grayish underwear, his face disfigured and bloody. The man was slamming his head into the wall. *Thump.* Pause. *Thump.*

In the cell on his right side, two people in white lab coats dragged in what looked like a person, though it was hard to tell from what he could see. Involuntarily, Max shuddered. He heard one of them say, "Elona was always so strong."

The lab coat guy looked up at Max, his eyes boring though the plastic walls separating them. "Soon it'll be your turn. We'll have fun together, won't we?" A greasy smile oozed from his face and made Max feel sick to his stomach.

Thump. Pause. *Thump.* The bloody man on the left continued butting his head against the wall. The lab coat guy broke eye contact with Max to yell, "Hey! Don't make me take your hat away again."

Thumping Man stopped. He reached out to the bed where a red knit cap lay. He picked it up, stroking it against his cheek. He didn't notice the blood from his forehead getting all over the cap.

Max buried his head between his knees, his shoulders—bony knobs and all—shaking.

Seventeen

T he Range Rover cornered better than she remembered, though the brakes seemed to need a little work. Mara shook her head a bit. Mick had slacked off on his maintenance schedule.

Hiroko gripped the shoulder belt crossing her chest, her fingers pressed into tight white fists. "I mean, it doesn't make sense. Why would he kick you out? You're a *Layil*." Her voice wavered as they took a very fast turn.

"Yeah, right. Whatever. If Momar can't find Max and the weirdo monks don't want me around, I've got no choice but ..." She'd promised Momar she wouldn't do anything, but Momar hadn't delivered on his side of the deal.

Hiroko's voice wavered a little, as if she really cared what happened to Mara. "The police will never believe you. You know that, right?"

Mara focused on the road for a second, remembering landmarks and street signs in the dense industrial district. Things looked different in a car. She pulled into a gravel lot in front of a mechanic's shop, parked, and turned the ignition off. "I'm not talking about the police."

Hiroko unbuckled herself and looked outside. "It's kind of a shifty area ..."

"Come on, let's go." Mara closed the car door behind her after she got out, and Hiroko did the same on her side of the car. "Just stay behind me. You'll be fine."

The unpaved parking lot held at least a dozen serious-looking motorcycles surrounded by an eight-foot chain-link fence broken only by a driveway. A red brick building sat at the back of the lot, divided into a garage area and a couple of standard-sized doors. In front of one of the doors sat a rotund man on a very-nearly-inadequate stool. Mara and Hiroko crept along the fence, hunched over. Then Mara stopped abruptly, hand held out behind her to stop Hiroko.

"How the hell is this possible?" she whispered. Mara had been about to stand up and greet the big man on the little stool when Momar rounded the corner and approached him first. "There's no way he could have gotten here this fast."

Hiroko said, "Yeah, well Abbot Greb has this, uh, power, and—"

"More Harry Potter crap?" Mara crouched lower, trying to become one with the chain-link, the gravel, and the weeds. She needed to change her plan, but she watched what Momar did first.

He had gripped the round man's hand in some odd way, which caused him to fall from the stool to his knees. Momar said, "I am very sorry. I did not intend to cause trouble. I need the door unlocked now. It is most important that I speak with Mick."

The fat guy flipped off Momar as the door opened with a bang.

Jackie came out and shook her head a few times. "Christ on a cracker, Momar, you could've just knocked." She looked at the man on the ground, who was shaking the hand Momar had dropped. "And you, Strabler, you should be embarrassed." Jackie motioned to Momar. "Come on in, let's see what was so damn important." Momar followed Jackie through the doorway, and the door closed behind them.

Mara looked back at Hiroko. "Okay, gotta go with Plan B."

Hiroko visibly brightened. "There's a plan? That's great. And Momar's here, so that's great, too."

Mara snorted. "Follow me." She crouch-crawled back along the fence, stopping at one side of the garage, where loud, off-key singing to what sounded like Led Zeppelin floated out of the open bay door. "Okay, I need you to distract the guy in there. Can you do that?"

Hiroko made a face. "What?" It was like Mara had spoken a different language.

"Shhh!" Mara crouched even deeper.

"Distract him. I don't know, act sexy or something." It sounded offensive and crude even to Mara, but she didn't have time to think of a nicer way to get to the point. She needed action.

Hiroko snarled her upper lip. "Oh, that's just gross! I don't even know why we're here, or what we're doing, or—"

Mara put her hand over Hiroko's mouth. "I need something in there. I need you to distract him, and I don't care how. You said you were in to help me and this is how I need your help right now."

She sighed. "And then I'll talk to Momar."

Hiroko brightened and said around Mara's hand, "Promise?"

A loud clang of metal on metal rang out from the bay door, and a burly voice yelled, "Dammit!" Hiroko's eyes got very large, and she shook her head back and forth. Mara shrugged her shoulders and pushed Hiroko out from their hiding spot into the opening of the garage door.

She stood there like a deer in headlights, motionless. Mara sighed and mimed walking in with her fingers. When that got no reaction from Hiroko, she made pushing motions, mouthing the word, "GO."

Hiroko shook her hair once and cleared her throat, which attracted the mechanic's attention. A male voice from inside said, "Who's there?" Heavy boot steps clomped toward the opening of the bay door, stopping a few feet from the threshold. "Well, now ... what've we got here? This here's private property, little lady. Y'all ain't supposed to be here."

Hiroko shuffled her feet a little and beamed a smile at the mechanic. "What can I say, I, uh, like bikers." She was trying for sexy but looked like a drunk, grinning marmot. "Are you a biker guy?" She walked into the bay toward the guy, disappearing into the garage.

Mara's chance had come. She edged around the corner and darted inside, hiding behind what looked like canisters of gas or air or something.

The guy said, "Sure I'm a biker guy. Wanna ride?" He walked

closer to Hiroko, who stood stock still. He reached out to her and took her hand. Hiroko made a small squeak, then grabbed his arm. The grin on his face disappeared as his eyes rolled back in his head and he collapsed like a bunch of wet laundry.

Hiroko looked around. "Mara?" Her head swiveled from left to right.

Mara stood up and waved at Hiroko. "What did you do to him?" She gestured at the pile of mechanic.

Hiroko smiled. "I just put him to sleep. He might have a few bruises, but he was a total creeper. He deserves it." She shuddered and brushed her arm where he'd touched her.

Mara shrugged again, her go-to response over the past several hours, and walked over to a lump covered by a gray tarp. She pulled the tarp away and grinned a little, revealing a sparkling Royal Enfield motorcycle. "I've missed you, baby." She pushed the tarp all the way off and touched the bike with reverence for a few seconds.

She turned to Hiroko, "You need to go. Take the Rover and go back to the monks." She tossed the keys to her.

Catching the keys, Hiroko said, "But you promised me you'd see Momar." Her frown was impressive.

Mara shrugged and grabbed her helmet off the back of her bike. "Yeah, I lied."

"I could come over there and put you to sleep, too." Hiroko crossed her arms, not making any move closer to Mara, who had busied herself strapping on the helmet.

"Yep." Mara fired up the bike easily, got on it, and drove out of the shop.

The gravel parking lot had one exit, and to get to it she'd have to pass right in front of the large bouncer on his stool. Mara revved her bike once, hoping it would have the power to make a quick escape. Strabler heard the engine, opened the door, and yelled something into the building. Moving much faster than she'd anticipated, he blocked her exit path with his considerable body. Mara pumped the brakes and power slid the bike around him, heading toward the row of Harley's. Maybe potential damage to these very expensive bikes would distract him enough to let her through. She circled around again, thankful to not see Strabler at the driveway anymore. She headed for the exit but found something familiar stopping her.

Mick.

Strabler's yell had been for Mick, who'd known just what Mara would do to get out. Mick positioned himself right in the middle of the exit, and though she hit the brakes hard, she couldn't stop all of her momentum. His arms grabbed the handlebars and absorbed the forward motion while his feet skidded over the gravel behind him, gradually bringing the bike to a full stop. While Mara was relieved she hadn't hurt him, a big part of her felt like throwing her helmet.

"Not today, missy," Mick said as he stood up and removed the key. One second too late, Mara grabbed for it, but he held it above her head. "Stop it!" he yelled at her. "You need to listen. This is real shit we're talking about here. You. Are. In. Danger. For once, you need to stop thinking about yourself. You're not gonna be able to help Max if you're gone. Or you're dead."

Mara slammed her fist on the gas tank, her frustration and anger getting the better of her.

Mick shook his head a couple of times and raised an eyebrow. "Wow. I've had her a year in perfect condition without a scratch. You get her for two minutes and ..." He made a tsking sound.

She felt nothing but the heat of anger and the chill of fear for Max. Scratches or dents could be fixed. Max might not be.

Eighteen

There had to be a way to find out where Max was being held. As Mara pondered the thought, she realized running away from Momar might be the exact wrong thing to do. He didn't seem all that surprised about Max being kidnapped—sad yes, surprised no. Maybe he knew who was responsible. She leaned against her bike, powerless without its key, and remembered the wind in her face and the freedom of being able to go wherever she wanted. It seemed like yesterday, except yesterday she'd been in an orange jumpsuit locked in juvenile detention.

Momar and Mick had their heads together, huddled so she couldn't overhear them. Hiroko pouted on the other side of the bike, her back turned to Mara as if she couldn't stand to look at her. Jackie, the bouncer-guy Strabler, and eight other bikers were sitting on their machines.

The two men approached her after their meeting, Mick looking a little pleased, Momar's face unreadable as always. Mick said, "It'll be fine."

"I must take her home. There is no other place we can keep safe, at least until the abbot allows her back." His voice was pitched for

Mick's ears, but Mara heard him. She always heard him.

"Look, ain't nobody getting in this time. We'll lock the place down." He nodded at Mara.

"But allowing her this ..." Momar pointed at the motorcycle. "I do not like it." Mara's heart beat a little faster in her chest.

"She needs something, man. It's been a rough year for her. And a rough day." Mick looked at Momar, who sighed.

Fifteen minutes later they were headed back to the Layil mansion. Mara was on the Royal Enfield with bikers on either side of her, two in front, and a pair behind. Momar and Hiroko were in the Range Rover, with Mick leading the pack on his Harley, and Jackie and Strabler riding tail. The entire procession drove at a snail's pace, but Mara got the wind in her face and a small imitation of the freedom of being a teenager for a little while.

Nineteen

Aeda loved candlelight. It warmed the skin and made small imperfections disappear, not that she had many. Sinioch didn't really care what kind of light was present in their chamber, as long as he could see enough to write in his books and enter his data.

The two of them sat at an ornate table, intricate carvings on the legs and the edges. Huge candelabras stood on the table and at the side of the room, dripless candles burning brightly. He dipped a pen into a pot of ink and wrote, his pen scratching into the vellum. Aeda glanced at the large man standing in front of them, his discomfort evident in every cell of his body. Another disappointment from another trusted underling, and in the same day.

"So. A young girl stopped you from completing your task." Sinioch never looked up but continued writing. Aeda saw his fingers whiten as they pressed the pen into the page, and his jawline tensed.

Tenoch touched the bandage on his face, which didn't quite hide the blush of embarrassment. His suit was creased as if it had just been unpacked, the black fabric a little shiny. "She had *power*. She must have Turned already. But we got the—"

Sinioch shrugged and continued writing. "She's only eighteen. And a girl. You're a professional *tracker*. Find her." He wasn't going to give Tenoch praise for doing half a job, but he wasn't going to punish him, either. A door clicked open at the far end of the room, causing Aeda to shift her attention.

She said, "We seem to have guests, dear." Someone important, or the guards wouldn't have let them into this private room. She hoped her husband got her subtext. Sinioch sighed, put down his pen, and stood up. Message received. He nodded at Tenoch, who gave a slight bow and slunk from the room.

There was a whisper of fabric as the person approached the table. The hooded figure came close, robes obscuring the identity of the visitor, though she had an inkling of who it might be. Aeda said, "Please show yourself." She hated surprises.

Abbot Greb uncovered his face and looked with his unseeing eyes at the pair.

Sinioch nodded slightly, his face remaining serious. "I've been told of the Layil child's disappearance." His voice gave off waves of concern.

He was so good even Aeda believed him.

At the abbot's side, almost appearing out of the shadows, were two Guards. One was a giant-sized Samoan man, the other a small Mayan woman. Both were dressed in black, and the candlelight glinted off the metal plates riveted into their throats.

Aeda startled a bit, glancing from one Guard to the other before collecting herself. She said in an even tone, "Surely a child is no cause to involve the Amyclaean Guard. We—"

Sinioch raised his hand to quiet her. "Please assure Armaros that my family is deeply disturbed by this, and that we are at your disposal." Sometimes his power was irritating instead of attractive, but she bit her tongue. She'd deferred to him for too long to stop the habit.

The abbot scowled. "Armaros looks to you, First Born—the Layils are of her line and she wishes for their safety. And for your help in locating the missing child." As if Sinioch needed to be reminded who was related to Armaros and what his duties were.

Aeda felt a flush of anger surge through her. She straightened herself, her shoulders held with pride. "It is not your place to direct us, monk." Sinioch looked daggers at her, his eyes promising discomfort and pain if she didn't obey. But she'd spoken the truth, and he knew it.

Sinioch said, "We shall spare no resource to find him." His voice oozed sincerity, and Aeda gave him credit for it. Sincerity was not something one counted on when speaking to a First Born. Especially Sinioch.

The abbot nodded. "If you hear or find anything, please send word to the monastery."

Sinioch bowed to the abbot, who turned with the Guards and left the room.

Aeda had not bowed. She would never bow to a monk or to Armaros's enforcer Guards.

Never.

TWENTY

Morning sunlight cut through the puffy gray clouds, beaming into the breakfast room at the Layil estate. As bright as the few rays of sun were, the silence made the room feel overcast and dark. No one spoke. Mara pushed a spoon through a yogurt container half-heartedly, her hair in spikes and dark circles under her eyes. Hiroko sat next to her, nibbling on toast and sipping tea while shooting side glances at Mara as you would to a teddy bear who'd turned rabid.

Dadima shook her head and dished more scrambled eggs onto Strabler's and Jackie's plates. They had the good manners to nod their heads in thanks.

"Mara, bad dreams are nothing to be—" Hiroko chirped before being shushed by Mara.

"Don't. Nope." Mara never looked up.

"I was glad I could help you get your breathing back to—" Hiroko tried again, and this time a hand shot out in the direction of her face.

"Stop. I'm fine. I'm fine." Mara's jaw twitched, and the spoon in the yogurt cup became a deadly stabbing thing.

Jackie had watched the whole exchange with eyebrows raised slightly. "I know how sucky this is for you, but we got this." She gestured toward the front of the house. "There are ten bikers on the driveway, three on the porch, and we've even got people along the perimeter." She sighed. "And I'm guessing there are people I don't know about, too." She shook her head and picked up her fork. "You gotta trust us."

Before Mara could say anything, Momar entered the kitchen and stood next to the four of them. Strabler took one look at Momar and leaned away from him, pushing his plate as far to the edge of the table as he could. Momar sighed deeply and looked at his young charge. "Please, Mara. Come with me." He gestured for her to stand up.

Mara looked up at him, her eyes narrowed. She thought about protesting. About swearing. About yelling in general. With a large exhale of breath, she opted to do what he said. "Fine."

Hiroko started to stand up too, but Momar stopped her. "No, please finish your breakfast." She sat back down, a slight pout on her face.

Mara hadn't been in her father's study for some time. She expected it to be dusty and dark from lack of use, but it was bright, clean, and sparkling. The sleek glass and chrome reflected every ray of light available.

After closing the door behind them, Momar turned to her. "I know the abbot told you some of the history of your kind, but he said nothing about your family."

He crossed to a chair and sat on the edge, watching her reactions.

She couldn't bear to look at him, not yet, so she turned her back to him and looked at the pictures and other items her dad had collected and treasured. "Whatever. He talked crazy-talk and then kicked me out." She shrugged.

"He spoke the truth."

"Again—whatever. It's not gonna bring Max back, or Mom, or Dad. Is it?" She was proud of the way her voice remained mostly steady. Ignoring him again, she noticed a rock sculpture she'd made when she was little. She hadn't realized her dad had kept it.

"I hope together we can do just that. But you need to know your parents had many secrets. For us to find them, and to find Max, we must understand those secrets." He cleared something out of his throat. "And some of those secrets will protect you."

Mara lost interest in her rock sculpture and heard Momar rise and cross to her dad's Mancala table. She rolled her eyes and reluctantly turned to face Momar. He reached out and picked up some of the small stones. "Uh, does my dad let you touch that?" she asked petulantly.

Momar nodded. "Watch." He counted a specific number of stones into one of the depressions, repeated it in a couple of others, then placed one stone in the end spot. There was a loud clicking noise, and the wall behind the table slid open.

Mara's mouth slid open, too. "Wow. That's kinda slick." Maybe her world was a little more woo-woo than she'd ever thought.

He led her into a small room, walls covered with drawers and shelves. The lighting was specifically designed to show off the items on the shelves—it looked like a museum exhibit. In the center of the room stood a carved wooden pedestal, topped by a leather-bound book, which looked disturbingly familiar.

"Hang on, is that like the monk's book? With the weird magic pages?" She didn't need anything else to have to cram into her brain. She felt full-up with crazy.

Momar shook his head. "No. This is called a Tracing, also known as a Record, which is a history of your family. Recorded by mine." His hand caressed the book, the leather oiled and old but immaculate.

She noticed something on the shelf nearby. A pair of dull-gray metal gauntlets, lit from above and below to show off the fine filigree of the metalwork, beckoned to Mara. She picked one up, and it gave off a shimmer of light when she touched it. "These are pretty sweet." She turned it and looked at it from all angles—it looked like the biggest and fanciest bracelet she'd ever seen. The glow seemed to get stronger the longer she held it. Must have been a trick of the light.

"Those are one part of a powerful relic set." He didn't outright tell her to put it back, but his voice made it fairly clear.

"Made from angel's wings, right?" The metal was lighter than it looked, almost warm to the touch. The glow increased. Mara wondered if Momar could see it, or if it was for her eyes only.

Momar smiled. "You did listen."

She shrugged. When she flipped it over again, it popped open like an invitation. She slipped her arm in at once.

He reached out to her. "No child—"

Before he could reach her, the gauntlet closed with a snap. Mara had meant to admire it on her arm, but the metal began to ripple and shift slightly, adhering to her shape and form. "What the ...?" She held up her arm and the gauntlet fit her like a second skin, as if it had been molded specifically for her. She reached up with her other hand and tugged at it, the skin of her arm stuck to the gauntlet like it was a part of her own body. "Get. It. Off."

Momar put a hand on her shoulder, and her breathing became more normal. "Find your center, like with *gatka*. Focus."

She took a deep breath, then exhaled. Mara closed her eyes.

"Now think of it opening, in your mind." His calm words assured Mara, and she thought of the gauntlet falling off her arm. She held the arm out, her eyes still shut. In a second or two, her arm got lighter, and she opened her eyes to see Momar had caught it and was looking at the metal object.

"What the hell is that thing?" She rubbed her arm where the metal had been, her skin a little cold.

"Legend says they are a very powerful weapon. But this—I've never seen them bind to the wearer—not even for your father." He continued to inspect the gauntlet. "He thought it was because the gauntlets are not of the Layil line. In fact, they are part of a powerful armor that was believed to be lost." He set the gauntlet back on the shelf with its mate and refocused on Mara. "He planned to show you this room, these treasures, upon your Turning. And now he is gone, and you are Turning far earlier than we ever expected." Momar sighed.

"The monk said that, too. What is Turning exactly anyway? Some kind of supernatural puberty or something?" She felt the gauntlets pull her toward them, like a magnet in her gut.

Momar ignored her, as he did most of the time. "He looked forward to sharing all this—your legacy—with you. There was fear, but also hope."

She backed up a step closer to the shelf. "They look really, really old. And it's like I can *feel* them calling me." Her skin felt empty and naked without the gauntlet. She wanted nothing more than to put them both on. She felt a strumming in her veins, and she knew it was the gauntlets.

He nodded his head, fingers gripping his chin as if he'd made some sort of discovery. "Fascinating. Your body and this relic speak to each other now." He rubbed his hands together a few times. "Well, there will be time for more information and lessons later. I wanted you to be aware of the room's existence. That done, I would like to see how your *gatka* skills have suffered during your—shall we say—absence." He gestured for her to follow him, then left the room.

Mara gave one last glance at the gauntlets before doing as he suggested. It couldn't hurt, and her skills were obviously rusty, or she would have kicked that kidnapper all the way to Seattle.

She and her brother were obviously not twins, but she'd always felt that she could send him the same kind of mental messages twins were supposed to exchange. And so in her head, she said, *"Hold on, Max. I'm coming. Stay safe."*

Twenty-One

The *gatka* training room was lined with tapestries and racks of weapons, some more deadly than others. An incense burner smoked lightly in one corner, the scent of cloves, patchouli, and other herbs floating here and there. Hiroko sat on the floor, her hoodie hunched around her neck, and stared at Mara. Momar stared at her too, no less intently. Her years of training came back after a few minutes of warm-up, the muscle memory taking over when she freed her mind and let things flow.

"Hiroko, are you familiar with *gatka*?" Momar asked quietly, his eyes not leaving Mara as she spun and kicked imaginary foes.

"Uh, I don't think so." Hiroko leaned forward a little, her eyes wide as she watched.

"It's a martial art developed by ancient Sikh warriors. It's a mind-body balance that melds with weapons training." He nodded his head as Mara continued her workout, her tank top sticking to her, her arms glistening with sweat. "Now it's time for the blade."

Mara stopped and caught her breath. "Seriously?" She panted a bit. "I'm still rusty. I might cut your arm off. Or mine." She panted some more and wiped her forehead.

He plucked a sword from the rack behind him, then picked an arm shield. "I'll take the risk."

Mara shrugged her shoulders, then picked out her own sword and shield. Once armed, the two of them circled each other a few times before separating and bowing once. Mara charged forward and clashed with Momar, who blocked her attack and spun away. They circled, attacked, parried, and sparred with the ease of people who knew each other well. It looked like a ballet, but with swords, shields, and a potential for massive bloodshed.

Mara had leaned in, blocked a cross by Momar, and spun around gracefully when the double door burst open with a bang. Strabler ran into the room and almost fell. "I tried to stop them ..." He sounded out of breath.

The two combatants froze, their eyes not leaving the other one until Momar gave a nod. Mara dropped her sword to her side.

Two people entered the room, all in black; one a small woman, one a very large man. They both had diamond-shaped plates on their throats, though Mara couldn't see how they were attached. Momar's eyes bugged out for a moment, but he blinked a few times to regain composure. Hiroko jumped to her feet, and both she and Momar gave small bows to the newcomers.

Mara looked from Momar, to Hiroko, to the strangers, confusion and questions crowding her mind.

"My Amyclaean friends, you are welcome in the Layil home." Momar gave another incline of his head to them, then turned to Strabler. "Thank you," he said, dismissing the biker.

The small woman nodded to Momar, then touched her chest. "Nin." Her voice could barely be heard, a painful, forced whisper. She nodded at her companion. "Semo." He didn't nod or bow but stood there with eyes focused only on Mara.

Nin stepped forward and handed Momar a scroll, sealed with a blob of red wax. Momar opened the scroll and began to read. Nin said, her face grimacing from exertion, "The child. Comes. With us."

The child in question looked to her guardian, shaking her head in denial.

Hell to the no.

Momar tore his gaze from the parchment in his hands, then looked at Nin and Semo. "Please give us a moment." He gestured for Mara to go over to where Hiroko stood. The two girls put their heads together for some semblance of privacy.

"Who are they? What are Ami-whosits?" Mara stage whispered. More clowns in the circus of her life, she guessed.

"Amyclaean Guards. Shhhh." Hiroko shushed her. "This never happens." The two of them looked over at Momar, who still studied the scroll. The Amyclaeans both stared at Mara.

"What never happens? And what's with the funny necklaces?" She nodded toward the visitors.

Hiroko gulped. "Uh, throat piercings." She pulled the strings of her sweatshirt until the hood bunched around her face, then slid down the wall until she was in a semisquat. Mara knelt next to her. "There are only twelve of them. They guard Armaros and ... uh ...

they …" She looked from Mara to Momar to the guards, then back at Mara, her eyes laser focused. "If you break certain rules in our world, they—" She made the universal throat-slashing gesture.

Mara got the message. Crystal clear. Had she broken some rule she didn't know about?

Momar finished inspecting the parchment, which he folded and put into his pocket. He walked over to Mara. "They have come to take you with them." His eyes were unreadable.

"You can't be serious." She couldn't believe the words he had uttered. Momar had just gotten her home, where he swore she'd be safe. And he'd sworn to find Max. And now he was going to ship her off with strangers?

"It is for your safety." His voice was even and calm. He turned to the Amyclaeans. "Because this is most unusual, I will need to speak to the abbot."

The woman, Nin, croaked, "We. Protect."

She and her companion moved toward Mara, who automatically picked up her sword and shield from the floor and jumped to her feet. "Like hell you will." Too much of her life was being dictated by other people—all she wanted was to find her brother and make sure he was safe.

She shook her head and assumed the stance she'd used when sparring with Momar. The Amyclaeans hesitated, and Mara used it to her advantage. She charged at them, her sword whirling.

Momar yelled, "No!"

Hiroko yelled, "Mara!" at the same time.

The Amyclaeans drew their own blades and parried Mara's attack. She continued to slash and thrust at them, wheeling away when she could. The two visitors didn't go on the offensive but continued their own defense. Mara pressed forward, backing the two of them into a corner, racks of shields and weapons nearby. The smaller one, Nin, saw a moment and used a leg sweep to bring Mara down. In the blink of an eye, Mara rolled from a sprawl back onto her feet, her sword held high over her head in preparation for a mighty slash. She screamed, "YEEAHHH!"

At that moment, another one of those bursts of power shot straight out from Mara toward the Amyclaeans. The two of them seemed to know what was coming and knelt to let it blow by them. The racks near them took flight from the power burst, weapons and shields crashing here and there.

Momar called out to the guards, "This must stop!"

The two Amyclaeans stood up and moved toward Mara, ignoring Momar completely.

Momar changed his approach and yelled, "Mara! Enough! Please, no more!"

Mara raised her weapon and drove forward into the two Amyclaeans, who easily blocked all her thrusts and slashes. She couldn't believe her guardian would let this happen, would stop her from defending herself from being taken who-knows-where. Her anger level rose, her slashes became deadly.

Hiroko ran toward the Guards and shouted, "She doesn't understand! You've got to—"

Semo, the male Guard, reached out with one hand and grabbed Hiroko. He pinned her to the ground, while his female companion continued to bat away all of Mara's best offensive moves.

Mara saw Hiroko in danger from the lunatics and felt something shift inside her. She prepared herself to make another attack when a shimmer of energy shot out in all directions.

The room seemed to freeze; the Amyclaean Guards assumed the positions of statues of battle, the male one pinning Hiroko, the female one with a knife raised. Momar was in mid yell, one arm extended.

It was like time had stopped for everyone but Mara.

Her next thought was to get out of Dodge while she had the chance, no matter how weird it was, and no matter how much Momar had assured her she'd be safe at home or safe with the Amyclaeans. She headed to the doorway, intending to leave, but bumped into Hiroko's leg as she passed. As soon as she touched Hiroko, something changed. Hiroko shook her head and stood up, the Guard's arm still pinning an imaginary foe. Mara looked around quickly, expecting everyone to return to normal.

Hiroko shook her head and looked at the continuing still life around her. "No. Way."

Mara shifted from foot to foot, her blood boiling with confusion and adrenaline. She tossed the sword from one hand to the other a couple of times, ready for the bad guys to wake up and start fighting again.

"You slowed time. This is like, wow. It's super rare." Hiroko was a master of understatement. She walked over to Momar and reached out to touch him.

"Don't!" Mara called out, one hand outstretched to stop her. She couldn't argue with him anymore. Not today.

Hiroko's hand snapped back, her head turning to look at Mara.

"I've ... I mean ... I gotta go." It might be a stupid and juvenile move, but she needed to be alone. If running away was the only way to be totally by herself, then she'd do it. For a while. And just in case, she kept the sword and shield as she ran from the practice room.

TWENTY-TWO

Mara stopped long enough at the front door to exchange the weaponry for a thin hoodie, a jacket, and a helmet, and looked out the window. The trees and shrubs near the house were motionless, even though she could see the wind blowing further out. A robin was suspended mid-flight above the front stairway. Strabler was fixed in a kneeling position in front of his bike, his hands extended but as still as everything else in Mara's time-bubble.

She started to formulate a plan, one where she got away from all the messed-up idiocy here and focused on finding Max and her family. In that order.

Mara opened the door, stepping out onto the porch. She threw the hoodie over her head, the material wicking away any residual glow from her workout.

Down the driveway a bit, Jackie was walking toward the house. She waved and said, "Hey girl, where you headed?" Her pace picked up, and she looked at Strabler with a funny expression before she was stopped cold, too—her body in mid-stride.

Whatever Mara had done, it was way frickin' cool.

Hiroko stepped outside behind Mara. "Please. You've got to go back. I know you don't understand, but all they want is—"

Mara shook her head. "I am NOT gonna be caged again." She walked over to Jackie and removed the knife strapped on her belt, careful not to touch any part of Jackie's body. She unsheathed the knife and walked over to the line of bikes parked there.

POP went the first tire and the second and the third. She continued down the line until all the front tires were flat on every bike but hers.

Behind her, Hiroko pleaded, "Please! Think of Max!" Her voice held as much persuasion as she could muster.

Mara spun on one foot to face Hiroko, her face flushing and her eyes shooting sparks. She had the knife in one hand raised in the air. Hiroko looked at the knife, fear in her stance and her face. Mara's anger faded a bit, and she tossed the knife into the grass. "They don't care about Max—they want ME! I'll find him. On my own."

She walked over to her bike, climbed on, and strapped her helmet into place.

"Mara, please listen to me—" Hiroko tried to follow her, but Mara cranked the bike engine and drowned out any sounds. With one glance at Hiroko and a shake of her head, Mara sped off down the driveway.

At the gate Mara stopped and looked back. Hiroko's shoulders had slumped in on themselves as she stood in the drive. And once she'd gone far enough away, her time-bubble had broken. She saw

Jackie fall to the ground, her body not prepared for the sudden lack of resistance when time went back to normal.

Mara didn't take the chance of the scary Amyclaean Guards making it outside to get her. She revved the bike and sped away from her house as fast as she could.

TWENTY-THREE

Rain never mattered much to people in Portland, and most of the skatepark was covered by the bridge so Ethan could skate anytime and not be constantly soggy. Sure, some of the street kids and homeless people hung out there too, but he didn't mind them. They had their lives and he had his. He finished a run through the bowl and did the trick he'd been practicing without wiping out.

"Woo!" He kicked the board up and caught it easily.

A man in a very dirty coat with a matted beard sat on the bench near Ethan, a medium-sized dog sitting by his mismatched shoes. Ethan sat down next to him with a smile on his face.

The man said, "It's been a while."

Ethan nodded his head, still wearing a crooked grin. "Yeah. Guess so. Been away."

The man reached down and scratched the dog's head. "Fox missed you." The dog raised his head to lean into the scratch. Ethan reached over to scratch him, too. A buzzing sound came from Ethan's pocket. He pulled his phone out to check it, which made his grin disappear.

"Girlfriend checking up on you?"

Ethan shook his head. "Nah, my mom. Gotta run. But it was good to see you. Later."

"Good to see you, kid."

Ethan stood up and grabbed his board, ready to climb down from the skatepark and get home. It wasn't that he wanted to go to their apartment or to see his mom in whatever state she was in, but he felt a responsibility to make sure she didn't hurt herself. Or at least keep the damage minimal.

Then he remembered he'd brought something. He pulled a granola bar from his pocket and tossed it to the man on the bench. "For Fox." The old guy caught it and saluted him, which made Ethan smile for a moment.

Probably not much smiling at home.

TWENTY-FOUR

Max's eyes didn't seem to be working the right way. After a few blinks, they were still fuzzy and not focusing. He tried to rub his eyes, but his arms were strapped to something. Something hard and cold. He looked around and could just make out a bag of blue liquid hanging over him. The man in the white lab coat stood next to him, his skinny face scrunched up as he checked the blue bag and the line leading down from it.

He noticed Max's open eyes and said in a singsong voice, "Tsk. Tsk. It's time for you to sleep."

With those words, Max felt his heart start beating faster, and his breathing increase. He turned his head to the other side and clearly saw a lady strapped to a table in another room past the transparent wall. She looked straight into Max's eyes and shook her head, her face exhausted and sad.

Max wished his vision was still blurry.

The prick of a needle poking into his arm whipped Max's head back to the other side. The white lab coat man connected the needle to the tube leading from the bag of blue stuff. Max looked around again, his voice not working and his body not responding to the "fight" commands he was sending. There had to be someone who could help him. It looked like an older man in a business suit stood just outside the door, and behind him a very old woman with long white hair, most of her face hidden by a hood. Max tried to make eye contact with them, but both looked bored—as if they saw little boys strapped to tables every day.

Where is my sister? Does she know where I ...

His arms and legs felt far away, his vision going a little blurry again. Max's head fell back to the side where the lady was strapped down. She still stared at him. He had barely enough energy to mouth the words. "Where. Am. I?"

She shook her head and closed her eyes for a second. "I'm. Sorry." She mouthed back to him.

That's the last thing Max saw before his eyes couldn't stay open any longer.

TWENTY-FIVE

It hadn't taken much time for Mara to ride down the hill to the skatepark. In a stunning reversal of her luck over the past couple of days, she saw Ethan doing a few tricks on his board. She could probably have talked to him there, but she opted to wait for him to head out. Once he left the park, she followed behind him a little bit. She knew the general area where he lived from what he'd told her at Cascadia, but not specifics. And since she knew where his neighborhood was, she'd been able to stay back and not be obvious about tailing him.

She felt kind of proud of herself.

As antsy as it made her to wait, she gave him ten minutes to settle in before she peeled off her helmet and walked over to his apartment building. The bricks had seen better days, the tree in front of it a stump. There were some colorful words spray-painted on the stoop, though the artist had neglected to make the words visually compelling.

Mara walked into the front hallway and found the door of Ethan's apartment. She raised her hand once, then let it fall. Then raised it again and knocked.

The door opened a few seconds later, a cloud of cigarette smoke billowing out with the words, "You got guts coming back here, you piece of crap." An older woman stood there, a glass of something in the same hand as her dangling cigarette butt. Her face was as lined as notebook paper. "Oh. You're not Ticker. Whadda ya want?" She slurred her words a bit, leading Mara to conclude what was in the glass.

"Hi. Uh, is Ethan around?" *This is not going well.*

The woman nodded her head, which wasn't really very smart. She lost her balance a bit and pointed her arm back over her shoulder. Her drink sloshed over the edge and splashed her, but she didn't notice. "Yeah. In back. Playing with his stupid games."

Mara shuffled quickly by Ethan's mom, the television blaring at full blast, the room's surfaces covered with magazines and papers. She nodded her head in thanks and walked to where his mom had pointed. There was only one door and it was closed.

She knocked once. "Ethan?"

No answer.

"Ethan—are you in there?" She knocked harder. This might have been a mistake.

She heard a couple of small metallic sounds, and then a voice. "What the ...?" His door swung open, and he stared at her as if she weren't real. "How? I mean, how did you find me?" He looked out into the hallway and winced at the mess, the noise, and his mom.

Mara entered the room and looked for a place to sit down. There were half-built computers and parts everywhere, along with a few skateboards propped on the wall and some energy drink cans stacked on one side. An iPad with a thick cord leading to one of the computers sat on the bed.

"Whoa. You raid NORAD or something?" She had never seen so much equipment in such a small space. Her grand plan suddenly seemed more and more ridiculous, like a bad cable movie. She paced a bit, not seeing anywhere to sit and needing to move.

Ethan raised an eyebrow, following her as she walked. "You'd be surprised how dumb teachers are about tech stuff and social media. They actually pay people to help them set up Facebook and Insta." He reached back and swung the door shut behind her. "So ..." He raised both hands up and smiled.

She didn't stop pacing, but actually moved a little faster. "I ... um ... need help." No eye contact, head down. How could she tell him everything without telling him anything?

He reached out to stop her, his hand gentle on her arm. "Already? You okay?" He turned her toward him and they finally locked eyes.

"Yeah, sure, I'm fine ..." She stammered a bit. "Uh ... do you have a T-shirt I could borrow? I had to leave my workout and ..." She picked at the hoodie material on her chest.

Ethan narrowed his eyes a little. "You came over for a T-shirt? Sure you did." He reached up into the closet and grabbed a laundry basket. "This is the stuff that's too small for me. It'll still be too big for you, but, hey—go nuts."

"Thanks. Turn around, okay? I'm shy." She made a fluttering

motion with her hands. Once he'd complied, she picked through the shirts in the basket, settling on an old Sex Pistols shirt with the sleeves ripped off. Mara shimmied out of her hoodie and damp shirt as quickly as she could, and then pulled Ethan's old tee over her head. It was dry and warm, and she instantly felt a bit more confident. Once the hoodie was back on, she knew she had to bite the bullet and ask him the hard questions.

It was a matter of what information to share.

"Okay, I'm good now. Thank you. I really appreciate it." She half-smiled as her stomach flip-flopped a couple of times.

"You're welcome. Anytime. Now why did you really track me down?" Mara opened her mouth once, but he stopped her. "And don't give me any BS about a shirt. You can talk to me. No judging."

She couldn't lie to him, but she couldn't tell him the truth, could she? Stuck in between, her shoulders slumped, and she sat on the edge of the bed, careful not to squish anything. "I ... I ran away and there are people after me and ..."

Ethan sat next to her. She leaned into him a little. "And I'm not sure where to go and—"

He interrupted her. "You're safe here. With me. I mean, you can stay here."

The weight in her chest lightened a little bit. "I dunno. I'm not sure. They might know."

He laugh-snorted, then shook his head. "Trust me, nobody wants to come to this building or this neighborhood." Ethan smiled at her, and the weight eased off a bit more.

"Thank you." She swallowed hard, hoping to hide the emotion and stress of the past few days, and leaned into him again in gratitude.

"You do move fast, don't you?" She heard the humor in his voice and turned her head to give him a laser glare. He chuckled then. "I mean in finding trouble."

Mara's defenses retreated again, and Ethan put his hand on hers, patting for a split second like you would a puppy, then resting his hand on hers. The warmth soothed her, and she knew she couldn't risk that. "Hey, no touching in group!" She pulled her hand out from his and smiled widely at him to make sure he wouldn't be hurt.

He smiled again. "Yeah, gotta admit I don't miss those sessions. I am never going back to Cascadia. Never." The grin left his face as he shook his head.

A kinship she'd rarely felt with anyone coursed through her. She studied him closely for a second, and then leaned over and kissed him. After a moment of surprise, he kissed her back. It was warm and soft and wonderful.

The sound of the front door being hammered and thrashed interrupted them. Mara and Ethan leaped to their feet and went to the bedroom door. Mara opened it a few inches to confirm what she knew in her heart—there were two large people breaking into Ethan's living room. And at least one, she could see, had been involved in taking Max from the fort. Ethan's mom weaved in front of them screaming and gesturing, but they pushed her aside like a cheap curtain. One of the men, the one she'd shocked with the taser, spotted her and shouted, "There!" The two bad guys headed toward Ethan's door, which Mara slammed and leaned against, hoping it would protect her for a few seconds. She balled up her fists, willing the weird powers she seemed to have inside to come out and help her.

Those are the bastards who'd taken Max and tried to take me.

Her blood felt hot, and her skin crawled with hate. A shimmer of energy left her body, then the world blurred, and things seemed to move in reverse. Ethan walked backward and went back to sitting on the bed. The energy shimmer moved from outside back into Mara with a thump, hitting her right in the midsection, and she doubled over with the impact.

When she stood upright, Ethan was on the edge of the bed, his eyes closed, his lips pursed. After a second of nothing touching him, he opened one eye and looked around. "Uh ... we were just ..." He shook his head. "How did you get over there?"

Mara looked around. "That was not what I expected. Hiroko would be flipping out." With a shake of her head, she remembered why she'd begged for the strange powers inside her to make an appearance, and they'd given her only seconds to get them to safety. She grabbed the dresser next to the door and tipped it over. It crashed to the floor, blocking the doorway. Ethan looked at her as if she were a lunatic.

"I know. But we've gotta go. Trust me. Take this, just in case." She lifted the iPad from the bed, pulling out the cable, and jammed it into the backpack sitting next to it.

Sounds from the living room indicated the front door had been broken down. Again. Mara pulled Ethan to his feet by the neck of his shirt and pushed him toward the window. "Go. I'll explain later." He flung open the window, his backpack slung over one shoulder, and looked back toward the door. Something big was coming down the hall toward them, his mom screeching and swearing at them to stop. Ethan made a move to go back and help but Mara stopped him. "She'll be okay. They're here for me. Go!"

A slam hit the bedroom door, which forced the dresser to slide a bit. Ethan was already partly outside, but turned and cried, "Grab my board!" Mara handed it to him once he was out of the window frame.

One more slam and the dresser skidded enough to let the bad guys push the door all the way open. Mara threw herself out the small window headfirst. She thought she'd made it but was stopped suddenly.

Someone had grabbed her ankle. The rest of her body flopped over onto the dumpster outside. She kicked both of her feet as hard as she could, trying to shake off the grasping hand of the kidnapper.

Mara's kicking managed to break the big guy's hold on her leg. Once free, they ran off as fast as they could. Mara hoped the scary people behind them in Ethan's bedroom would give up and go back to wherever bastard kidnappers congregated.

Yeah, right.

TWENTY-SIX

Sirens wailed in the distance as Tenoch looked over at Tala, both men stopped at the bedroom window.

"I touched her. Skin to skin." A slick smile spread over his face.

Tala responded with the same expression. "Excellent."

TWENTY-SEVEN

Ethan took the lead in their flight from the apartment. He dashed down alleys and made sudden turns here and there, Mara right on his heels. After one turn, he pulled up abruptly, his hands on his knees, and Mara almost ran into him. He was out of breath and panting.

2, 3, 5, 7, 11, 13

He cycled through a sequence of prime numbers.

Out of breath herself, Mara said, "What are you doing? Come on."

He stood up and walked in a little circle, stretching. "They won't find us here."

Mara pulled on his arm. "They will find us. It's what they do. You do not understand these people ..." *Who am I kidding, I don't understand them, either.*

He broke Mara's grip and pulled a phone out of his pocket. His fingers moved over the screen quickly, then he raised it to his ear.

She rolled her eyes. "The cops won't come."

Ethan moved the phone away from his face. "I'm not calling the cops." He turned and walked a few feet away. Mara paced in the alley, waiting for him to finish. Sounds of a loud angry voice came out of his phone, leaking around his ear. He mumbled something into it, pressed the screen, and put it back into his pocket.

"She's okay. Mad, but okay."

"I told you she would be. Now let's go." Mara turned, ready to resume their flight but he grabbed her arm.

"Where exactly are you going to go?" His voice seemed irritated. And he had every right to be.

"I'm gonna go get my motorcycle." It seemed the logical thing to do—get something that could put miles between her and those creeps who had tried to grab her. Her plan didn't have much else besides "motorcycle" and "Ethan," but she didn't want to admit that.

Ethan shook his head. "Whoever attacked us back there followed you to my place. You probably don't want to go back for the bike." He shrugged his shoulders.

A couple of swear words and one small foot stomp later, Mara realized he was right. She hated it, but he was right. She hoped the neighbors didn't know what a Royal Enfield bike was or what it was worth, or it would be skeletonized in fifteen minutes.

"Okay ... you said you ran away." His voice was patient but sounded right on the edge.

She nodded. "I did. Those people at your place, whoever they are, they ... they took my little brother." She swallowed hard.

Ethan face telegraphed his disbelief. "What? I don't—Did you call the cops?"

She shook her head. "No. Look, I can't call the cops." Her voice broke a little on the last word. She grabbed Ethan's hand and looked into his eyes. "Please. I know it makes no sense, but you've gotta trust me. I don't ... I don't have anyone else. And we've got to get out of here. Please."

Ethan stared into her eyes for a second, then sighed. "Okay. I know a place we can go. But you have to tell me what the hell's going on ... okay?"

She nodded her head and threw her arms around his neck to hug him. Relief surged through her. He would help. He would listen.

It feels good to have an ally. At least I have one.

Twenty-Eight

T he row of motorcycles stood in a line in the garage, all of them sporting completely flat front tires. A flatbed truck was parked near the front door, Strabler backing another flattened chopper off the back. From the passenger seat of the Range Rover, Hiroko watched Mick, Jackie, and the mechanic she'd put to sleep repairing the flats. Jackie checked a tire on a balancer, the mechanic guy raised a bike up on a lift, and Mick just stared at the Rover as it drove up, whatever job he'd been doing forgotten.

Momar parked and stepped out. Hiroko followed suit.

Strabler looked at Momar with a shake of his head. "That girl of yours is a piece of work." He wheeled the bike he'd off-loaded into the repair bay, still shaking his head. Hiroko wanted to defend Mara, but she couldn't.

Hiroko and Momar entered the garage, and the mechanic took one look at Hiroko and his face went a brilliant shade of scarlet. He mumbled something under his breath about getting coffee, never letting his eyes leave Hiroko as he tried to back away from her.

Hiroko chirped, "I'm sorry?" She fluttered her eyes at him. "Not really." She mouthed at him soundlessly.

He stumbled over a toolbox, causing a wrench to fall with a metallic clanging sound. The mechanic turned nearly purple and practically sprinted out the door. Hiroko would have laughed under different circumstances.

Momar faced Mick and Jackie, who were still repairing tires as best they could. "We cannot find her. She seems to have vanished." He took a breath. "I hoped your methods might have turned up a lead?" He faced Mick, hope in his voice if not in his expression.

Mick stood up and wiped his hands on a rag. "Well, it's only been a few hours. I've put feelers out, but ..." He shook his head. "But I'm pretty sure we know who has the boy."

Hiroko looked from Momar to Mick, surprised Mick knew anything at all. "How do you know—"

Momar interrupted her and spoke to Mick. "We cannot accuse a First Born of such a thing without proof."

Hiroko circled back. "Wait, he knows about—"

Mick interrupted her this time. "For a year, you've tried to find who kidnapped Paul and Veronique. And they're still gone. This time, you can't wait. He's only a kid." His impatience and anger were tempered by as much respect as he could muster, but Hiroko saw Mick's jaw clenched after he spoke.

Momar had seen it, too. "Do not lecture me. I am the Layil's Scribe, and I know—"

Hiroko stomped her foot twice to get Momar's attention. "He knows about First Borns? About Offspring? He ... he knows about us?"

A lifetime of secrecy and now this biker is spouting off about her world like it was an everyday walk in the park?

Mick's jaw unclenched enough for him to smile at Hiroko. He reached into his back pocket and pulled out a flask. "Yeah, I worked for Sinioch for a while. And then for Paul. I've seen more crazy shit than anyone would ever believe." He raised his flask in a mock toast and took a drink from it.

Hiroko's mouth dropped open, her eyes blinking in disbelief. Words tried to form, but she only stammered a few syllables.

"Calm yourself. We could not operate in the world without some people learning what we are." Momar patted Hiroko's shoulder. She looked from Momar to Mick again.

"Yeah, I know enough to know I don't want to know any more." Mick took another drink.

Hiroko pointed to Jackie, who'd put down her wheel and had placed a cigar between her lips. "What about ... what about her?"

Jackie lit the cigar, then puffed once. "Don't worry, Hello Kitty. I keep my head down and my mouth shut." She smiled at Hiroko.

"You have only recently Turned. There is still much for you to learn. Please, for tonight you must listen." Momar gave a small nod of his head to Hiroko, who nodded back and sat down on a stool. Her shoulders drooped as much as her pout. She didn't like it, but she would wait and pay attention. It's why she'd excelled at her studies as a healer.

Mick set his flask on the workbench and grabbed his leather coat. He looked over to Jackie, who nodded and followed suit. To

Momar he said, "Got a few scumbags I need to visit. Find out if anyone's seen anything. Keep your phone handy."

Momar's hand reached out and stopped Mick from leaving. "Take Hiroko," he said.

"What?" Hiroko and Mick said at the same time. It was hard to tell who was more surprised.

Mick's jaw clenched again. "That's not how I work. No one rides with me." He shook off Momar's suggestion.

Momar took a deep breath and explained, "If you find Mara, she will run. She has lost trust in us. But she still trusts Hiroko, so you will need her." His voice stayed calm and even. "I can only hope to convince the Amyclaeans that we can find her peacefully and bring her in. Then we can search for Max. But if we do not bring Mara in tonight, the Amyclaeans will locate her using their own means. And if she battles them again ..." Momar shook his head sadly.

Mick's expression hadn't changed a bit. He shook his head too, but his jaw was set, his mind made up. Hiroko had to admit that Momar's idea was a sound one. She didn't blame Mara one iota for not trusting anyone.

Momar looked at Jackie, who looked at Hiroko, then Mick, then back to Momar. "Oh. Oh, hell no. Not me. I don't want Sailor Moon on my bike, either." Hiroko shrugged her shoulders.

"Guess that'd work." Mick nodded his head.

Jackie threw her cigar on the ground and stepped on it. "Christ." She went over to her bike and straddled it.

"Don't I get a say?" Hiroko chimed in.

She would much rather ride in a car than on a motorcycle, but mainly she wanted to help Mara and to reunite the Layil family.

"No." Momar and Mick said at the same time.

For the first time, she wished her Turning would have involved weapons.

TWENTY-NINE

T he giant dumpster was pulled right next to the back wall of the old brick high school. With a jump and a scramble, Mara and Ethan were on top of it and almost eye level with the first floor. Mara could see a vent window cracked open slightly. It was all the opening Ethan needed. Within a few minutes, he had pulled himself inside and opened a bigger window for her.

"I think Momar knows, but he wouldn't tell me. He's scared," she said as Ethan extended a hand to her.

"Momar? Is he the Arab dude?" He pulled her up and helped her over the window ledge.

"Indian. He's a Sikh. He's uh ... umm ... he's my Scribe." She brushed the dust from her pants as they stood in a dark hallway.

"What's a Scribe?" Ethan motioned her forward and she followed him down the hall.

"I always thought he was like a butler or something. I've known him forever. But I guess he's more like a guardian and protector." She wished he *could* protect her, but those days seemed gone.

While Ethan strolled calmly down the middle of the hallway, Mara slunk against the wall, her hands behind her as she tiptoed behind him. Ethan turned to look at her once, shook his head and said, "Kind of like your Alfred, huh?"

She shook off the reference. "Aren't you worried about guards or cameras or anything?" She continued her spider-like adherence to the wall, whipping her head back and forth.

Ethan shook his head. "Nah. Budget cuts. And there haven't been night guards here in years. It's a bad area and a bad school. Nobody cares." He shrugged and stopped at a doorway. Reaching into his pocket, he removed a ring of keys and jangled them a few times to find the correct one. He smiled a little, then inserted it into the door where it popped the lock easily.

He opened the door, motioning her inside as if he was some kind of usher or maître d'. "What they *do* have here is bandwidth. Tons of bandwidth."

Mara entered the room but stuck to the wall near the light switch. Ethan looked at her like she was bonkers and passed by her to sit at one of the tables, facing an old, beige cement-block of a computer. "Oh yeah, pipe galore." He flipped a few power switches.

She closed the door gently, easing the lock mechanism into place with a gentle click. "What's pipe? Sounds kinda creepy."

He shook his head. "So I used to run this lab when I was in school, which is why I still have a key. And pipe just means speed. Bandwidth. Same thing." He pulled his iPad from the backpack and connected it to the big beige computer. A few clicks on a keyboard later and screens were flashing on both devices. He paused to look up at Mara, then back to the keyboard. "Okay. Tell me everything that happened yesterday. Don't leave anything out, even the tiny details."

Her head tilted to one side. "Uh, why?" She'd crossed to stand next to him, and she watched the monitors flash. She didn't know what she was seeing, but it looked impressive.

Ethan's focus remained on the screen in front of him. "Everything is just data and patterns. The trick is knowing where to look and what queries to run." He stopped the tapping and focused his attention on Mara.

She took a few steps—pacing was her thing when stressed out. "When I asked you for help, I don't know what I thought you'd be able to do. But this ..." Mara shook her head. "If you hack into—"

Ethan was on his feet in an instant and next to her. "Look, what I did—what landed me in Cascadia—it was bad. It hurt people. I was stupid. But maybe this time I can truly help." He raised a hand as if to put it on her shoulder, then awkwardly dropped it to his side.

"But if you're caught, you could go back. Right? They could send you back?" She spun to face him and looked into his eyes.

After a flash of acknowledgement and a sigh, he sat back down at the computer, his hands poised over the keyboard. "Just tell me everything you remember."

THIRTY

The armor covering his chest and back shifted subtly to the contours of his body, as if he'd forged the relic himself. Sinioch loved the feel of the metal, a slightly warm, almost living thing. His heart beat with a stronger cadence, his lungs filled with purpose each time the armor touched his skin.

Moonbeams and city lights shone through the glass dome of the ceiling, illuminating the empty room with a depth not achieved by standard lighting. The intricately inlaid wood floor was smooth beneath his feet, the benches around the perimeter empty except for one shadowy figure huddled on one side.

He closed his eyes and brought his hands over his head, then in front of him in a standard prayer-like pose. "We must train to be strong. To be ready. To remind ourselves what we are and what we should be." He nodded, and the shadowy figure of the Puppeteer melted into the darkness.

Sinioch's eyes opened, his senses reacting to everything around him. "Ever the cautious wraith, aren't you? Watching. Slipping from shadow to shadow. But a shadow is weak and has no power. Your reliance on—"

A blur, like a wisp of smoke, rippled past the air in front of Sinioch, only to disappear again. He spun on one heel, then looked down. A glowing red gash appeared in the armor on his chest. He smiled as the armor mended itself, shifting and adjusting until the mark was erased as if it had never occurred. "Very nice. I see you've procured a relium blade."

He continued to move through the space, not seeing the Puppeteer but prepared for another attack. Sinioch knew his exterior looked like a normal middle-aged man, but he still moved like a tiger: deadly, every muscle movement with purpose, and with blinding speed when the need arose.

From a dark corner, the words hissed like a snake, "Ssssurely my time here ... hidden away and caged ... drawssss to an end."

Sinioch turned to follow the words, and each syllable seemed to come from a different quadrant. She was a formidable training partner, one of the reasons he hadn't disposed of her. But that changed nothing in his plan. "That would not be wise. You are hunted still, my wraith."

A sibilant scream echoed off the glass of the dome, followed by a push of air near his side. Sinioch ducked and parried the blade of the Puppeteer, who screeched her anger. She attacked again from the other side, and he spun on one heel, his heightened senses telling him where she would be.

He was First Born. He was limitless power.

And he deserved nothing less than to be treated like the demigod he was.

THIRTY-ONE

Ethan's head snapped up after focusing on his iPad screen for a few minutes. "Wait. Say that part again."

Mara shook her head a little. "Uh, what?" What had she missed? She'd told him everything she could.

"You said something about a taser on a stick? Something like that? And Momar said ...?" He looked at her as if every syllable could save the world, his eagerness to find something—anything that would help them.

"Yeah, Momar was really keyed into it. The name on it ..." She tapped her forehead, willing herself to see the shock stick in her memory. "It was like the guy who invented Super Mario ... Miya ... is it Miyamoto? Morimoto? Something moto?"

He snapped his fingers and swung back to the computer, his fingers blinding as they typed.

"There." He pointed to the screen. Mara leaned over his shoulder to read.

"I have no idea what I'm looking at." Mara shook her head. It meant nothing to her, but she was glad he thought it was important.

"It's the shipping manifest from the Port of Portland. Shows all the ships that have entered the port in the last two months." Ethan scrolled down the list, looking carefully at each line of data. He stopped. "Bingo."

Mara looked at the line he pointed to, reading it. "Miyamoto Industries."

"Looks like the cargo was delivered to a private storage facility in the industrial section near the docks. Uh, about a month ago." He turned to Mara and smiled.

"But that could mean anything. Or nothing." She shook her head. *He is cute, but how does this help us find Max?*

"It's all about patterns. Or in this case, a deviation from a pattern. According to their website, Miyamoto is a Japanese munitions company. Sells non-lethal riot control gear, mostly to Eastern European and African countries. Portland is neither of those."

He raised an eyebrow, his voice getting a bit more excited. "And then you get jumped by bad guys with a shock wand from a company that's supposedly never shipped any product to Portland before."

Mara shook her head again. "Couldn't someone have just bought it somewhere else and transported it here?"

"The website says it's a brand-new product. And looks like it's not officially allowed in this country yet." Ethan smiled a little bit and then went back to the keyboard, switching tabs, and bringing up more windows.

"So who brought it here? Who ordered it?"

"Again, that's the weird part. Deviation from the norm." He tapped a few more keys. "Can't find any record of a name on this shipment. Just customer numbers. It's gonna take time to go back and break into their system to connect those customer numbers to an actual name. And even then, we'll be lucky if it isn't some dummy corporation." He kept scrolling and typing.

Mara felt the skin on her arms tingle as if a charge had gone through her. Her head twisted to one side. "Do you hear that?" She craned her neck from side to side, sweeping the air for sounds.

Ethan looked up and said, "What?" As soon as the word left his lips, Mara had slapped a hand over his mouth.

A second later, the door to the lab crashed open. One of the kidnapper bad guys in the lead, maybe Tala, closely followed by the guy built like a tank, Tenoch—the one Mara'd tasered at the fort. Ethan yanked the cable from the computer and jammed his iPad into his backpack. He looked at Mara, who screamed, "Run!"

He shoved a couple of tables across the aisle to block the guys from getting to them. He slung on his backpack, dropped his skateboard to the floor, and jumped on.

Mara willed the powers she'd experienced to make a return again, her fists balled up with effort and her face scrunched in concentration.

Nothing. Dammit.

Ethan yelled, "Come on!" When Mara didn't move, he pushed his skateboard around her to intercept Tenoch, the guy built like a tank. He dove off his board and went into a full baseball slide while picking up his skateboard. As he slid into Tank Guy, he hit him full force in the crotch with his board. The guy dropped like a rock. *Impressive move, really.*

The other man, who'd been circling around the other side, called out to him, "Tenoch?"

Ethan popped up, grabbed Mara's arm and yanked her away. He pulled her to the door, and the two of them raced into the hallway.

The tank guy, Tenoch, must have had some kind of steel underwear because when Mara looked back, the two men were not far behind.

Mara stopped and turned toward her pursuers as Ethan kept running. She screamed at them, all her frustration and pain funneling through her body in one wave of emotion. "AAAAAAGGGGGGGHHHHHHH." For Max, for Ethan, for herself, for her parents—everyone they'd messed with.

The power burst from Mara in a wave that ripped all the doors off the lockers in the hallway, and blasted Tenoch and the other man back into a wall, knocking them out cold.

After a second, Mara walked closer to them, surveying the damage. She glanced down the hallway, then looked down at the crumpled human shapes, assessing them for potential threats. They seemed neutralized, at least for now.

Ethan walked back toward Mara, dumbfounded. And not for nothing. It looked like a bomb had been detonated in the hall. Locker doors swung from broken hinges, paper fluttered to the ground like huge snowflakes, and the bad guys were in a pile.

Mara looked at him, a little smile curving the corners of her lips, her head cocked to one side.

Ethan stared at her. His mouth still open in amazement. She shrugged, and walked toward him, her gait calm and steady.

That'd teach the bastards to mess with Mara Layil.

THIRTY-TWO

The hag mocked him in her anger. Sinioch knew that sparring with and baiting the Puppeteer was dangerous, which was precisely why he'd done it. He felt a drop of sweat roll between his shoulder blades, his attention on the dark and shadowy corners of the room.

With an abrupt slam, the main double doors were thrown open. Sinioch spun toward the intrusion, his hands balled into fists. "What???" Orders had been disobeyed, and someone would pay.

The light poured in from the outside hallway, obscuring his vision. The smooth sound of his wife's voice carried to him. "Tenoch has found the girl." His mood instantly changed from anger to satisfaction. She told him not only what he wanted to hear, but why she had intruded on his private training time. Aeda understood order and rules. She understood him. She was a fitting partner.

He stood straight, dropping his arms. "He has failed before." Sinioch ran one hand down the smooth armor on his chest, his heartbeat returning to normal. The feel of the relium on the skin of his palm both comforted him and made his blood sing.

From the shadows, a hissing noise arose. "Sssssend me for the girl." The Puppeteer's hooded face appeared at the edge of the light.

Aeda spun on one heel to face the old woman. "Know your place, wraith." She turned back to Sinioch. Her voice smooth again. "Tenoch will not fail again, now that he knows that—"

"The girl has Turned. Yes. With the Amyclaean Guards involved, however, matters are complicated. He must use great caution." Sinioch reached out and ran one finger down Aeda's silken cheek. She really was beautiful. Ageless and beautiful.

She practically purred. "Soon we won't have to care about the Amyclaeans. Or Armaros. Or the Covenant." She raised her hand to Sinioch's and brushed his fingers with hers. Sinioch smiled at her and nodded. One corner of her mouth raised slightly, then she turned and left the room.

He took one more deep breath, and whirled around, striking the Puppeteer with a well-placed kick to the center of her chest. She flew back into the wall, her shadows absorbing most of the blow.

The power felt sure and right coursing through his veins.

THIRTY-THREE

Being a lab technician sucked. Especially at this place, with this weirdo scientist experimenting on people. If he wasn't being paid a stupid amount of money, he'd be gone. Easy enough to think about, but heavily armed guards and the not-so-subtle threats of what would happen if he violated his nondisclosure agreement had made his career choice a permanent one. The tech reached over the fat, nearly naked dude to refasten the arm restraint that had come undone. Being a barista would have been so damn much easier.

Weirdo scientist liked to talk to his subjects, too. He leaned over the man on the table, pressing a hand to the nearly naked guy's chest. "Our time together has ended." His voice was a bad imitation of a villain in a cartoon. "And your progress has been most enlightening for the study."

The subject bucked and strained against the restraints, making the tech's job even harder. He grabbed again for the straps, failing to get them connected and ratcheted properly. Weirdo scientist always made the job harder as soon as he opened his mouth.

A beep behind the tech made him turn his head for a second. He went back to trying to fasten the restraint and heard a brusque female voice say, "Prepare for the girl's arrival."

The scientist responded at once. He loved to hear himself speak. "Excellent news. And what about—" A second beep signaled the end of the communication. The tech could hear the smile in the next words. "Soon we'll have another guest." If there was a school for evil scientist tropes, he'd graduated at the top of his class.

The strap wouldn't go into the end of the fastener, and the man on the table kept moving around. The tech reached across the man's body to try to restrain him with his own body weight, which he realized was a mistake two seconds too late.

The subject reached up with his free arm and put the tech into a headlock, one sweaty bicep curled around his neck. The tech pulled at the arm choking him, but it was futile. He struggled to breathe, clawing at the flesh of the nearly naked guy. The man was very big, even after being subjected to experimentation and torture for weeks.

The last thing the lab tech heard was the scientist yelling, "No! Don't make me take away your—"

And his world ended.

THIRTY-FOUR

Elona sat on the floor of her cell, leaning against the clear wall so she could talk to the boy. "It sounds like a fun game." The wall also helped her to sit up. Being in the lab had not gone well for her or any of her various body parts.

Max sat on the other side of the wall, his hair messed and dark circles under his eyes. "It's not too hard. My dad taught me when I was little." He sniffed and wiped his nose with the back of his hand, the bandages apparent under his sleeve and on his hand.

"Maybe you can teach me to play sometime?" She knew it would never happen, but she felt responsible for keeping the boy's spirits up, at least for now.

The door to the outside lab room opened, and Elona and Max sat up in surprise, then cowered back into the wall. Instead of the white-coated monster, a very large man clad only in grayish boxer shorts stumbled in, his arms bloody and his eyes wild. He lurched to his cell door, but it wouldn't open. He began to bang his head on the door, his eyes locked on something inside.

Max stood up and looked around. He turned to Elona. "What's happening?" His voice quivered.

For the first time in what seemed like forever, Elona felt a glimmer of hope. She craned her neck to see past the open doorway and spotted two bodies slumped on the floor in white coats. She smiled at Max. "It's okay, hang on." She turned her attention to the large man. "Hey!" She repeated it a few times.

The man finally looked up from his head banging. Elona pointed to the touch pad on the outside of the door. "Use the pad to open the door." She mimed pressing buttons with her fingers. He cocked his head to the side, a confused expression on his slack face.

Being direct wasn't working. She tried another tactic. Elona pretended she was putting a hat on her head. "Hat? You want your hat? Push the buttons." She pressed imaginary buttons in the air. Motivation came in many forms.

The man looked at the touch pad for a moment, then slammed his huge fist into it. Sparks jumped from the pad, and the door to his cell opened. The door to Elona's cell partially opened, too. He walked into the cell and grabbed the red hat, which he pressed to his cheek.

It wasn't a huge victory, but she didn't care. It was something. She struggled to her feet, her injuries hampering every movement, and squeezed out of the doorway. She turned to Max's cell door, which had opened only a few inches. "Help me, little guy. We can get it open."

With both pulling, pushing and kicking, the door wouldn't budge. Max put his face into the opening and began to cry. Elona's heart ached for him.

"Hold on, Max. Hold on. I'll come back." She pressed her face to his and squeezed the fingers he managed to get through the crack. He continued to cry, shoulders hunching with defeat. "I'll get help. I promise. But I've gotta go out to do any good. Okay?" She squeezed his fingers again.

He nodded his head a little bit, tears coursing down his dirty cheeks. He let go of her fingers and slumped down onto the floor, scooting back into the farthest corner.

Elona hobbled out into the lab, the dead body of the lab tech crumpled like a pretzel, the scientist knocked out cold but still breathing. She passed them both and tried to remember how many guards were on the other side of the main door. Two? Three? More? With her good arm, she grabbed the most lethal-looking scalpel on the tray of instruments and took a deep breath.

The door slid open with hardly a whisper, the guard on either side standing at attention with their eyes forward. They had been well taught. It gave Elona enough time to slice one throat, then the other. Both slumped to the ground. She'd been well taught, too. She pulled the security card from one of their coats and dragged them into the lab through the open door. It made a mess, but she didn't care.

Broken arm or not, she was a lot stronger than she looked.

THIRTY-FIVE

The MAX train was nearly empty as it traveled through downtown. It was late, after all. Mara and Ethan sat hunched over near the doors, Ethan's iPad on his lap, his fingers tapping and swiping.

Mara asked, "What's that?" She pointed to the image on the screen.

"A map of the port. It's kinda huge. There's no way we'll find the private storage area unless we—"

Mara grabbed his arm. "Whoa. You're not going to the port with me. Nope."

He looked at her like she was bonkers. "What?"

"It's too dangerous. I don't want you to—" She couldn't complete the sentence.

He shook his head, then rolled his eyes. "Look, these people know where I live. What I look like. And they'll figure out I hacked into the shipping system, too."

Mara dropped her hand. She'd forgotten about all those things, about the seemingly unending power and resources these people had. Enough to kill, steal, and kidnap with no repercussions.

Ethan looked into her eyes. "Mara. Come on. What happened back there?"

She couldn't make her eyes stay on his. She shook her head. At the time she'd felt like an avenging goddess, but now ...

He kept going. "I mean, in my room something happened, too. It was like someone hit the rewind button on reality. And then ... the hallway. You blew up the hallway in the school. That's not normal, is it?" Ethan stared at her, one eyebrow raised in a question.

Mara pivoted and moved to the seat behind them, not able to meet his stare or explain things away. If she told him, she endangered him. She wasn't about to put the only person helping her into the crosshairs again.

He followed her movement, turned in his seat to face her and continued. "I'm totally in the dark here. And it's a weird dark. Like creepy-red-eyes-staring-at-me kinda dark."

She shook her head again. "I know. I'm sorry. But I don't know ..." Mara took a deep breath and looked up to face him. "All I know for sure is that I'm scared. Really scared. But I have to find Max— he's all I have left. The rest, well ... I just don't know." She exhaled. It was the best she could do.

Ethan patted the hand she'd put on his seat back. Mara looked up. "Okay." He patted her fingers again. "Come back up here and sit with me."

Mara stood up and took her seat next to him again. Gratitude flowed through her, something she hadn't experienced much lately.

She smiled at him. *He really is the best friend ever.*

"Yeah, well, we may need help." He tapped a couple more times on the iPad.

She nodded. "I know."

Thirty-Six

The port area where Ethan took them was enormous. Massive steel shipping containers were stacked like building blocks, some five containers high. Mara felt like an ant in a Lego playset. And even though it was late, there was activity here and there as people off-loaded cargo from ships docked at the riverside. Mara heard the whir of machinery behind them and pulled Ethan by his backpack into the space between two containers.

Ethan looked at her after the forklift had passed them. "Thanks. I'd better check where we're headed." He shrugged off the backpack and pulled out his iPad. After a click and a swipe, he showed the screen to Mara. "See? We're close." He pointed to a small square on the iPad, then around the corner to a building.

That was all the incentive Mara needed. She peered around the container, saw the building and took off at a run.

Another forklift rumbled to life in front of her, and she dashed behind a parked truck while it passed by. Ethan joined her a few seconds later, breathing a little hard and glaring daggers at her. "Seriously? You couldn't wait a minute?" He panted a few more times.

Mara ignored him. She looked at the front of the building where she'd been headed—two armed guards stood by the entrance, silver shock wands hanging from their belts.

"Dammit. Look." She pointed to the guards.

"Definitely your taser-stick-thingies, huh?" Ethan blew a long breath out. "I think we should go now."

Mara looked over at him like he was crazy. "What? No way. We need to find out who they are and what's in there." She tried to think of things that would distract the guards, besides blowing them up or making time go backwards, which she had zero ability to handle with any kind of precision.

Ethan put a hand on her arm. "Look, I thought this would be easy. Break in and find out who's buying the taser sticks. But this—" He gestured to the guards, their shock wands, and what looked like real guns in their holsters. "This is different. We should bail. I only need a little time to hack that customer number and then we can—"

Mara cut him off. "Shhhh ..." She pointed to a large black SUV driving up to the building they were watching. The guards stood at attention as the car stopped just past them. Tenoch, the tank, and the other big man, Tala, stepped out.

"Crap." Ethan had a definite way with words.

With a huge sigh, Mara pulled her cell phone out of her pocket. "I really hope Mick isn't too mad at me." She pushed a few buttons and put the phone back in her jacket.

As they watched, Tenoch and Tala put their heads together,

sharing something. Suddenly, Tenoch looked up and swiveled his head like a radar dish, settling on precisely where Mara and Ethan were crouched behind the truck. "Tala. She's here." He made a motion with his hand, and Tala took off toward them at a run.

Mara and Ethan glanced at each other and headed the other direction, the maze of containers making it hard for them to see where they were going. As long as it was away from the scary dudes, it seemed the right way. They rounded a corner and saw an opening, heading toward it without saying a word. Halfway there, the two security guards stepped into the space, their hands on their shock wands.

Mara and Ethan skidded to a stop, intending to turn a different way. Mara said, "Get behind me." But when Mara looked back, she saw Tala coming for them like a freight train.

Under his breath, Ethan said, "Not any better."

The guards reached for the wands and switched them on. The tips glowed.

Mara made an instant decision. She grabbed Ethan's hand and ran straight for the guards.

Ethan yelled, "What are you doing?" as they barreled closer to the taser sticks.

Mara yelled back, "Trust me!" One of the guards charged forward, a smile on his face. The footsteps of Tala behind them sounded closer and closer.

Mara felt the power this time, felt like she could direct it and make it do what she wanted. It started as a warm sensation in her belly, then spread out to all her extremities. As the guard had almost reached them, and Tala closed in from behind, a wave rippled out from Mara. Exertion forced a sound from her she'd never heard before. Time stopped around them.

Everything and everyone around them froze in place.

Ethan was still moving forward and almost ran into her. "Wait ... what? How is ...?" He looked at the guards stopped like statues, shock wands extended. There were even tiny blue bolts of electricity visible on the tips of the wands.

"Let's go!" Mara tugged on his hand. The weird power had worked with her this time and she felt it flow through her veins, warm and strong and sure. It wasn't an aberration; it was a part of her. Maybe someday she could learn to control it, to master it, and decide which direction it took.

Someday.

Ethan's face was both amazed and afraid. "But ... but ..."

"Okay, this is *so* not normal. It's crazy, I know. But now's not the time to go into it. I'm not sure how long this lasts, and we've got to run ..." She pulled his arm toward the opening between the guards.

"So you *did* blow up the hallway, too." Ethan was putting things together. He stopped to look at the guards, and the blue lightning bolt perched on the tip of the taser. "Wow."

Mara saw that Tala was frozen behind them, and she peeked around the nearest container to see Tenoch immobile, too. The sound of tires screeching around a corner hit her, and she felt a load drop off her shoulders. "Ethan, he's here. Thank God—"

Before she could finish, Ethan had reached out to touch the outstretched hand of the nearest guard. Mara screamed, "NO!"

Instantly, the guard dropped out of the time-freeze and back into real time. He smacked Ethan to the ground with one fist and charged for Mara. She stepped backwards as quickly as she could, but the shock wand touched her, and she crumpled to the ground.

THIRTY-SEVEN

Momar had seen everything unfold in front of him, since his car had been caught in Mara's time-freeze as soon as it got close enough to her. He could do nothing to stop Ethan from touching the guard and nothing to stop Mara from getting shocked. As soon as she was unconscious, the time-freeze stopped, and everything went back to normal. Momar stomped on the brake pedal just in time to prevent him from hitting anything.

As Momar braked, Tenoch raised his arms over his head and a bolt of lightning struck near the Rover, sending chunks of asphalt into the air. A second bolt hit near the front of the car, forcing Momar to pull the steering wheel to one side to avoid being struck. He stopped the car just short of slamming into a container.

Ethan stood up, shaking off the effects of being punched. "Over here, dick wad." He taunted the guard, motioning him to come forward. He'd forgotten about Tala, who tackled him from behind, sandwiching Ethan between the ground and his large bulk, knocking all the air from his body. With the boy down and gasping like a dying fish, Tala stood up and headed toward Tenoch, who was focused solely on a now-conscious Mara.

Momar growled, opened the car door, and reached into his jacket for his blades. As he exited the vehicle, he heard Mara's voice taunting Sinioch's enforcer.

"Hey, scary dude," She called out to Tenoch, his hands raised over his head to threaten her. Mara bent over a little bit and then stood straight up as a blast of power left her body and fired straight into Tenoch, who collapsed in a heap. She staggered and leaned against a nearby container. Momar was both impressed and frightened of her power, but his desire to protect her overrode everything.

Must. Protect. Mara.

Both security guards faced Momar and his blades. He assumed his normal fighting position, the same one he'd taught Mara all those years ago. His blades whirled, stopping each attempt to use the shock wand on him. He parried each thrust, never giving the guards the opportunity to unholster their guns and fight back. One guard dropped, his chest a blur of red stripes. The second guard followed suit, his throat slit from Momar's blades.

Momar wanted to look around for Mara but was interrupted.

Tala charged Momar, a shock wand in his fist. Momar spun and whirled, stopping the shock wand from touching his body. Tala was bigger and stronger, but Momar had his blades and speed.

Tala dropped just as quickly as the two guards had.

Momar saw a blur out of the corner of his eye—it was Ethan, up again and hurtling on his skateboard toward Tenoch, who seemed to have recovered from Mara's power blast. Momar shook his head a bit, knowing that Ethan's charge was the equivalent of bringing a dandelion to a gunfight. As soon as Tenoch saw Ethan, he raised his hands, and a bolt of blue lightning ripped the ground open in front of the skateboard, sending Ethan and his board straight into the side of a container, the boy crumpled into a heap. Mara screamed, and from the sound, Momar knew she was only a few feet away. She had been coming to help him.

Tenoch turned to Mara and Momar, his hands lifted in the air again. Another blue bolt struck the ground near Momar, asphalt and rocks shooting up from the ground. Momar took a few steps closer to Mara, his knives held at the ready in front of him. Two more bolts struck the ground between Momar and Mara, closer than the first.

The urge to protect her surged through him like a wave. She was Layil. He was her Scribe. He had trained her, raised her, loved her—even though she may have thought otherwise. She was the culmination of his family's service to the Layils and his reason for being. She may have been a pain at times, but it hardly mattered now.

Must. Protect her.

With all the strength in his body, Momar hurled both his blades at Tenoch. At the same time Tenoch raised his hands. Momar hoped he'd stopped him in time. He stepped sideways in front of Mara. A searing heat entered Momar's chest, his body wracked with electricity.

He dropped like a stone.

Must. Protect ...

THIRTY-EIGHT

Mara had helped Ethan as much as she could, but when he slammed into the container, all she could do was scream. The blasts of blue from Tenoch's hands were scary, but nothing was scarier than Momar calmly dispatching the people who were trying to get her. She watched him expertly fight and deal with the guards, and Tala, and she expected Tenoch to go to his reward just as quickly.

Momar had thrown his blades at Tenoch with deadly aim. They sunk into his chest with hardly a sound, just as a bolt of blue left Tenoch's hands. Tenoch dropped to his knees, blood bubbling from his mouth. His words carried to her. "He's ... just ... a Scribe?" he whispered just before he fell over.

She turned to Momar and saw him flat on the ground, a scorch mark on his chest.

He'd stopped the bolt meant for her.

He'd protected her as he always had.

Mara's center exploded, and a scream ripped from her throat as time slowed down around her. She knelt down and tried to raise him up but could only get him wrapped into her arms.

Tears began to flow down her cheeks.

Momar's eyes opened. He looked up at her and raised a hand to her face. "I've ... I've failed."

"Shhh ... we'll get a healer ..." She felt an overwhelming sadness, tempered with a burning rage.

His hand dropped. "Your power—" he blinked a couple of times "—more than you know." His voice was nothing more than a whisper. His eyes closed.

Mara's attention was broken by a familiar sound coming from behind a row of containers, breaking her power over the time flow. The rumble of motorcycles made tears flow harder, but she didn't let go of Momar.

Mick, Strabler, and Jackie pulled their bikes up next to her. Hiroko jumped off the bike from behind Jackie and rushed to kneel beside Momar, throwing her helmet off as she ran. She laid her hands on his chest and closed her eyes.

"Please help him. Do something." Mara pleaded with Hiroko.

Momar's eyes fluttered open. "Save the Layil Record... give it to the abbot." He grimaced and his eyes shut again. Hiroko opened her eyes and looked at Mara. Momar said, "No. Go to Ethan ... I can hold on ..." He whispered. His breathing ragged.

Hiroko's gaze went from where Jackie stood next to Ethan to Momar. He managed to nod his head to affirm his statement. Hiroko stood up and ran over to Ethan.

Once Hiroko had gone, Momar coughed and blood seeped from the corner of his mouth. "Your family's secret—"

She stopped him. "Don't say anything. Wait for Hiroko to come back. You'll be fine." She tried to smile at him, but it felt like a grimace of her own.

He coughed once more, fighting for the words. "It is your … destiny." He exhaled once, and then his muscles went slack, his eyes blank.

Mara's head slumped to her chest, tears flowing freely now. The rage she'd felt before was washed away with pain and grief. She'd lost something she hadn't known she had. A friend. A protector. Family.

In the distance, she heard sirens.

THIRTY-NINE

H ey, guys. We've gotta get outta here. Now." Mick's voice bounced off the metal around them. Even though Mara hadn't raised her head, she imagined that Mick had surveyed the bodies, chunks of pavement, blood, and various weapons lying amid the containers—and had an idea of how it would look to police. Mara couldn't see the scene anymore through her tears, but she still knew he was right.

Jackie and Hiroko looked up from Ethan and nodded. Jackie scooped up Ethan and headed for the Rover. Hiroko ran to Mara's side.

"I am so sorry," she said to Mara, putting a hand on her shoulder. Hiroko's tears matched Mara's. Mick came over and gently pried Momar from Mara's arms, lifting his body as if it weighed nothing at all.

Mara continued to kneel, her head slumped over, her shoulders heaving. She realized her arms were empty, and she looked over to where Tenoch laid, blades sticking from his ribs. Anger boiled in her, a heat she couldn't control. She rose in one motion, crossed to his body, and kicked at him with all the fury in her. That wasn't enough, so she kneeled and beat the corpse with her fists. Her hand caught the edge of his jacket, and a flash caught her eye—a security badge with the word TransWorld on it. She screamed into the air, "I will find you!" Her sobs echoed off the walls of containers.

Mick came over to her, trying to pull her toward the car. She knew they had no choice but to go, but her grief and anger fought him. "No. NO! Who are these people? And where's Max??" Mick enveloped her in his arms. She kept screaming, her fists pounding on his chest.

He hugged her as tightly as he could. "We gotta go, but I promise you this ain't over." He took a step toward the car, Mara forced to follow within his arms. One big step at a time, he walked them to the Rover. The sirens sounded much closer.

Mara saw Ethan in the back seat, Hiroko next to him laying her hands on him for healing. His eyelids fluttered, which made Mara as happy as she could be. She began to get in the passenger seat, then stopped. She ran back to the motorcycles, stopping at Jackie's bike, and put the helmet on.

Mick crossed to her. "What're you thinking? We gotta roll NOW."

Mara adjusted the strap under her chin. "I've gotta get something from my house. Momar ..." her breath caught to say his name out loud. "Momar said it was a weapon." All the things he'd ever said to her played on repeat in her mind, their importance now carved into stone.

Mick shook his head. "Nope. Too dangerous."

From the back seat of the Rover, Ethan got out and stood up. Unsteady, but on his feet, he said, "Well, maybe not. I mean, we took out all these guys, right?" He waved at the bodies around them. "So isn't it going to be a little while before whoever sent them figures out we got away?"

Mick considered this for a second and then nodded. "Okay. That actually makes sense. Jackie and Strabler, get Momar's body back to the monastery. Ask for Abbot Greb. Tell him what happened." He cleared his throat a couple of times. "Mara, whatever we're looking for, it better be worth it. We've gotta be in and out fast." He nodded to her and went over to his bike.

"Wait!" Hiroko jumped out of the Rover and raced over to the motorcycles. She started to get on behind Mara.

"No way." Mara stopped Hiroko. She shook her head.

"I've got to get your Record and keep it safe. Momar told me I had to." She sniffed.

"Record?" Mara knew it sounded familiar, but couldn't remember why, which bothered her.

"You know, the big book? Really big, really old book? I have to find it." Hiroko nodded her head.

Ethan raised his hand. "I'm coming, too." He snagged helmets from the back of one bike and handed one to Hiroko, keeping one for himself.

Mick slapped his helmet. "Jesus Christ! You've got to be—" He growled. "Kid, a few minutes ago you were in no shape to be standing up. Now you wanna ride?" He shook his head again.

"I can ride. It's just sitting down." He put the helmet on.

"Dammit. Get on the back." Mick couldn't argue. "Jackie, take off. Strabler, follow her. Hiroko, behind Mara. Kid, you're with me." He craned his head to one side, listening as the sirens closed in.

FORTY

Jackie sat on a simple wooden chair in a room that was anything but simple. Shelves lined every available space on the wall, crammed full of apothecary jars, tincture bottles, boy-band trinkets, and stuffed animals. A picture frame covered in small cartoon monsters proclaimed, "Hiroko is our Best Fan Ever."

She held a toy model in her hands, turning it back and forth, marveling at the intricacy of it. Jackie wasn't an anime fan, but she'd look at anything to take her mind off the body lying on the table two feet from her. She looked over at Strabler, who stood near the doorway and was pointedly staring at a spot on the opposite wall.

Neither of them wanted to face the grim reality in front of them.

A very old monk came in, a black shawl in his arms. As Jackie watched, he tottered over to the body and spread the shawl over Momar, covering the face and torso. He sighed once and shuffled out the door.

Voices outside were muffled, but Jackie heard someone say "Abbot." She rose from her chair and tucked the figure back onto the nearest shelf. Strabler turned to the door, too.

Abbot Greb walked in, his face grim and lined. He held up his hands to Jackie and Strabler, as if to quiet them in a room already deathly still. A few steps later, the abbot laid his hands on Momar's chest. His head dropped, and he murmured something Jackie assumed was a prayer. With a heavy sigh, he finished and looked up at her.

"Follow me." He nodded at her and turned his attention back to Momar's body. He put his hands in a prayer position, then touched his forehead, his heart, and his forehead again, a gesture Jackie found oddly moving. She stood up and followed him from the room, Strabler right behind her.

He turned to her in the hallway. "Momar's death has proven his suspicions were true." He looked up and down the hall, making sure they were alone. "It's Sinioch."

Jackie nodded. "Yeah, that's what we thought."

"Now Max is in even greater danger than Mara. I must find the Amyclaeans ... and send them to Sinioch's tower."

She said, "What would you have me do?" Jackie wasn't the most hard-core Layil employee, but she'd liked and respected Momar. It seemed fitting to offer.

"I'm afraid for now, the Amyclaeans must find and rescue the boy. We must protect the girl. Bring her here. It is her only hope." He bowed to her slightly. She bowed back.

Jackie nodded at Strabler, who gave her a thumbs-up. Ironic— since she was pretty sure nothing was going to be okay ever again.

FORTY-ONE

It felt wrong to be in the house with all the lights out. Like she was a burglar in her own home or in some kind of weird fever dream. Mara followed closely behind Mick and Hiroko, Ethan trailing after her, the hallway easy to maneuver as long as she kept a hand on the wall.

Having a task to complete meant she didn't have to think about Momar. Or the lightning-bolt-firing asshat who'd killed him. Or Max.

A sigh escaped her. She obviously failed at the "no thinking" thing.

Mick stopped and opened the door to her father's study. "All right, we're here. Now go get what we came to get." There was just enough light for Mara to see him gesture for her to go in. Not enough for her to see the impatience that must have accompanied the gesture.

She crossed straight to the Mancala table and grabbed a handful of the small stones. Only then did she realize she had a problem. "Crap. I don't remember the sequence." She closed her eyes and tried to see it in her mind. *What had Momar done?*

Ethan touched her on the shoulder. "What do you mean, you can't remember?"

Mara pursed her lips. "It's a secret entrance. You put the right number of stones in the right cups and—" she points to the wall "—it's supposed to open."

"Are you kidding me? You said Momar showed you ..." Mick's voice rose a bit, his annoyance now obvious.

"No, I said he showed me the gauntlet thingies and the book. *He* opened the secret bat cave." She felt her cheeks flush and grow warm. *Why do I never remember important things?*

"And you based this whole trip on THAT?" Mick was definitely pissed now. He'd moved beyond annoyed. "Do you realize the kind of danger we're—"

"I hate to interrupt a good fight, when we're supposed to be all stealthy and stuff, but uh ... d'you mind if I give it a try?" Ethan had a smile on his face, the first one Mara had seen in what felt like forever. He reached for her hand, uncurling her fingers from the seed stones, letting them drop into his palm.

He leaned over the table, looked up at a painting on the wall, then down to the Mancala game and the pits carved into it. Counting carefully, he dropped a few stones into one pit, then another, then another. A *click* emanated from the wall, and the table and wall rotated open.

Hiroko said, "Oooh!!" Her hands came together in a tiny golf clap.

Mara's jaw dropped open. "How ... How'd you do that?" He continued to amaze her.

Ethan shrugged a little. "I keep telling you, life is all about patterns." He pointed to the painting. He nodded his head and looked around at the others. "Really? You don't see it? Nobody?"

Mara looked from Ethan to the painting of a landscape, back to Ethan. "What?"

Mick clapped one of his hands on Ethan's shoulder. "I don't care how you got it. Guess you're not worthless, after all. Let's move."

Recessed lighting activated as Mara stepped across the threshold of the secret room. All the hairs on her arms stood straight up as soon as she was close to the gauntlets, and she stripped her jacket off and handed it to Ethan. "It's amazing ... I can feel them." It was like her body was telling her how familiar it was with the metal; that it was a part of her, and she a part of it.

Ethan made a face. "What?"

She pulled the first gauntlet from the shelf and slipped it onto her wrist. As soon as it came into contact with her skin, a sigh escaped her lips.

Mick peered over her shoulder. "Those are super weapons? They look like jewelry to me." He looked over at where Hiroko was oohing and ahhing over an old book.

Mara grabbed the other gauntlet and put it on. There was a sound in her head, almost like a lock clicking open. Hiroko picked up the book, carrying it over to Mara to see.

When the gauntlets were both in place, the metal shimmered and became liquid-looking, molding and adjusting to her forearms before settling back into a solid piece. She shook her arms a bit, but they didn't move.

"Ooh, that is so cool," Hiroko said next to her.

Even Mick looked a little impressed. "Yeah, okay. That ain't no costume jewelry."

Mara took her jacket back from Ethan and put it on. "There's one more thing I need from the house. Some insurance. Let's go."

Forty-Two

The motorcycle clubhouse was mostly dark, the city around them quiet in the evening. At the back of the empty bar, a single light shone on the oak surface of a table with six people seated around it. Jackie stood at one end, pouring a green-labeled bottle of Irish whiskey into three glasses. Ethan pointed to himself in question, and his reward was a laser glare that should have singed off his eyebrows. He raised his hands in a no-harm-no-foul gesture.

Mick looked up from his glass. "I don't care what the old monk says, she stays with us for now." He sipped the amber liquid. Jackie had already told them what Abbot Greb had said, and who he'd named as the person behind the violence.

Jackie nodded and passed a glass to Strabler.

Mara pulled something out of her pocket and set it on the table—it was the TransWorld badge she'd taken off Tenoch's body at the port. She stared at it, the light reflecting from the laminated surface. "So we know where to go now. And I say we go there. It's gotta be where Max is and ..." her voice caught, "we've gotta get there before ..." She stopped.

Mick reached out to pat her hand. "Yeah, we know. The crap at the docks confirmed it." He sighed and slowly drained the rest of his drink.

Mara nodded and put the badge back into her pocket. She swung around to head for the door when Hiroko stopped her.

"Are you kidding? Sinioch is a First Born. You don't know what that means. He's super, super powerful. If he's got Max, let the Amyclaeans handle it. It's what they do. They're the closest thing to superheroes in our world. They're the best. And that's what Jackie said, right? The abbot's sending them to get Max." Hiroko put her hand on Mara's arm, concern on her face.

Mara blinked once. "That's all well and good for the freaky-monk dude, but how do I know he'll do what he said?" She shook her head, her jaw clenched. "The Ami-whatchers didn't care a bit about Max when they came for me. They don't care about him like I do." Her voice wobbled, but her gaze was steely.

Hiroko got up and stood in front of her, blocking Mara from passing. Mara thought about all the pushing and shoving she'd seen and experienced at juvie. She thought about Max being scared and alone. She thought about Momar and his patient teaching year after year. Her blood burned for action and revenge.

"Let. Me. Go." She felt a glimmer of her power in her abdomen, but it was cut short by Ethan putting his hand on her back. She took a deep breath and shuddered a little at the thought of what she could do, even to a friend.

"I'll go with you. We'll all—" he motioned with his hands "—go with you. But you've gotta give us some time. You can't just walk into this place and demand your brother. We've gotta be smarter than they are."

Mick stood up. "He's right. We'll all go. But there's a way to do these things. And barging in the front door ain't the best choice."

Mick picked up the Tullamore Dew bottle and poured himself another, then raised his glass. Strabler and Jackie raised theirs in response, and Ethan and Hiroko put their hands in. All five of them looked at her with determination, intelligence, and not a little fear. She felt her irritation melt away and admiration took its place.

"Okay." She swallowed and nodded. "And thank you. All of you." Mara made eye contact with each person. For Momar. For Max. For all of them.

Mick threw back the last of his whiskey for a second time and slammed the glass onto the table. Strabler and Jackie followed suit. "Just like old times, friends. Let's DO this." He shook his head like a lion straightening his mane.

Ethan piped up, "Okay, I'm gonna need a few things ..."

FORTY-THREE

Aeda stood over their chief scientist, her three large guards a hair's breadth behind her. She glared at him even as he bled all over his white lab coat.

If wishes were knives, this man would have been impaled thousands of times over.

He crouched, holding his face together, cowering before her.

"Sinioch is very displeased. As am I." The words were choked out around her intense anger and loathing. She turned from what was left of the man and spoke to the guards.

"You. Put the blue IV bags into that trunk." She pointed to a stainless-steel box sitting on the floor. "And you two. Put that man, the one with the red cap, into the stasis pod. And for the love of all gods and goddesses, use the straps to secure him." She sighed. She remembered a time when their guards had known exactly what to do and hadn't needed to be instructed in every minute detail.

The scientist whimpered a little, his hand raising as if he wanted to be called upon. "We will discuss your issues later. Get yourself—" she sniffed and waved a hand at him "—fixed up and help them prepare that wretch for transport. I leave for Japan in an hour. We have subjects and data to move." Aeda spun on her heel. Their plan was so close ... so close to coming to fruition.

She hated dirty work almost as much as she hated incompetence.

FORTY-FOUR

S trabler struggled under the weight and bulk of the computer equipment in his arms. Ethan grinned a little, watching the older man sweat and swear as he stumbled into the club, cords dragging behind him.

"This is the last of it." Strabler exhaled noisily. He wiped his forehead with his arm. "My van could hardly hold all of it. I'm not even gonna ask how you paid for everything." He shook his head.

"It's better that way." Ethan nodded. "And thank you." He started organizing and stacking the boxes and cubes, attaching cords and cables as he went.

Strabler watched him, his head shaking. "Your mom is a piece of work, by the way. After she screamed at me and threatened me, she tried to hit on me."

Ethan didn't even slow down. He kept working on the setup, his hands constant in their movement. "Yeah, that's my mom." He shrugged a bit.

Mara walked up and dropped a duffel bag on a nearby table. "You've got an hour, okay?"

"Okay. I've got a lot to do, but if I get some help, I can—" Ethan continued working but looked up to see how she'd react.

"Don't count on it." Mara walked away toward the door. "One. Hour."

FORTY-FIVE

Mara slid Momar's blades into her backpack, handles stuck out for easy access. She hesitated a little bit, touching them reverently. Momar would be proud and afraid, encouraging yet wanting to keep her safe.

The different sides of her mentor had never made sense to her before, but she got it now. He'd always wanted her to use her gifts wisely and for the good of the world, but he'd also taught her to ride a bike, to dance, to fight, and to defend herself. He had raised her, almost more than her parents, and she felt his loss in every cell of her body.

She sighed and put the pack on her back. She walked over to the tables near the bar, stacked with equipment, power cables, and monitors. "Okay, Ethan. What'd you find?"

He smiled up at her. "I've got the schematics of the TransWorld tower and the tunnels under it. It's rough, and might be an old copy, but it's better than nothing." He stood up and disconnected his broken iPad from the rest of the computers. He loaded it into his backpack. "Screen's cracked from when I fell on it, but still works. Got everything downloaded onto it."

Jackie handed Mara an earpiece, then went around and handed one to Mick, Strabler, Hiroko, and Ethan. "They've all got fresh batteries. We should be able to communicate with each other as long as you keep it in your ear." She inserted hers and shook her head a few times. "Might be a little feedback-y since we're all so close."

Mick patted the saddlebag hanging over his shoulder. "Got the armory right here. Jackie's got one already on her bike. We can distribute when we get there."

Ethan sipped an energy drink, his feet tapping with nerves. He looked over at Jackie, who had raised the hair off her neck to adjust the earpiece and revealed a small bird tattoo. "Nice ink." He pointed. "On your neck." He nodded and smiled again, his fingers strumming a rhythm on the can.

Jackie sighed. "Kid, you gotta lay off the Red Bull. Seriously. Your heart's gonna explode." She put her hair back down and patted her ear. "Good to go now. And I could use a drink. Strabler?"

Strabler popped up and ducked behind the bar for another bottle.

Ethan looked at them and shook his head. "Yeah, like booze is gonna help us."

Jackie turned to him, one eyebrow raised. "It's not gonna hurt." She took a sip at the tiny glass Strabler had poured her.

Mara watched each of them and took a deep breath. She zipped up her leather jacket, picked up her helmet and placed it under her arm. "Ready?"

"You know this is impossible, right little girl?" Mick looked at Mara and shrugged.

Mara shrugged, too. It was definitely impossible. But so were all the things she'd made happen over the last 48 hours. So were First Borns. So were Offspring. So was having your little brother kidnapped. All in all, her whole world seemed impossible.

She looked straight at Mick. "I dunno, I kinda like our odds."

Forty-six

Amyclaean Guards never seemed to walk anywhere; they managed to glide on noiseless feet. They were taught to be soundless, a lesson each novice learned over and over until it was done correctly, Nin thought. One of many lessons drilled into them during their training, most of them painful and reminding them what an honor it was to serve Armaros.

And so Nin and Semo simply were there. No noise. No warning. Even though Semo was roughly the size of an NFL offensive lineman.

The night watchman at the TransWorld tower spit out some of his coffee when they appeared in front of him with no warning. Nin had to stop herself from rolling her eyes.

"Sinioch," she said in almost a whisper, yet also a command.

"Holy shit! Who the hell are you?" He stood up, liquid dripping from his chin. "And how'd you get in here?"

Nin rasped again, "Sin ... i ... och." Each syllable was excruciating, but she emphasized each one as if the watchman was mentally challenged.

The guard reached under the desk with one hand and grabbed the weapon at his hip with the other. "I don't know what your deal is—" he extended the shock wand and pressed the button, blue waves emanating from the tip "—but it's time to get you two back to whatever circus you came from."

Semo extended one arm over the desk and grabbed the watchman by the neck, lifting him up and over in one movement. While in the air, the guard's flailing arms touched the wand to Semo's barrel-like chest. Semo blinked twice and threw the night watchman against the wall, where he collapsed into a heap.

Nin nodded at him, pleased. He wouldn't have been her first choice for this assignment, but he'd come through in a pinch. He'd done well at the Layil estate fighting with the girl, and he'd done well now. It wasn't their fault the girl had begun her Turning early.

Now they could continue their search through the building.

They had their orders. Nothing would stop them until those orders were fulfilled.

FORTY-SEVEN

Ethan and Hiroko stood next to Strabler's van, watching Jackie try to pick the lock of a chained gate leading into an old building.

"It's basically a spiderweb of tunnels under the old parts of the city. Shanghai Tunnels, man. It's how the smugglers used to move illegal stuff around." He pointed to his iPad screen. "See?" A map was displayed under the cracked glass.

Hiroko peered at the diagram. "I thought that was a crazy, urban legend thing."

Ethan raised his palms and shrugged. "Its true most of what you hear is BS the chamber of commerce makes up for the tourists. But it looks like there's maybe a kernel of truth in the old stories. Some of the tunnels do still connect to modern buildings." It'd been a hunch that had paid off. He was glad for a small victory—he didn't want his only purpose to be some bad guy's punching bag. A dude could only take so many hits before he started to doubt himself.

Mick and Mara walked up to the van. "There were three guards at the loading bay, but two of them went inside as we watched," she said, and then shook her head. "Don't know why. There's still one guard outside, and who knows how many inside." Her face was set and serious. She had put aside her grief over Momar in favor of her quest for her brother.

Mick looked over at Jackie. "Any luck yet?"

She didn't turn to him, just kept working on the lock. "It's a real bitch."

Mick gently pushed Jackie aside, then kicked the gate, breaking the lock.

"Son of a ..." Jackie muttered.

"Just a little stubborn." Mick waggled his eyebrows at her.

Mara squared her shoulders and was the first one through the gate, just as Ethan had expected.

FORTY-EIGHT

Nin and Semo were surrounded by TransWorld guards, each guard holding an activated and glowing shock wand. They'd only made it as far as the extended lobby before being confronted by more of Sinioch's employees.

"Sinioch," Nin said again, her throat burning with every word.

Two more guards with wands joined the group, bringing the total to six.

"Sin … i … och." She said again. Semo stood next to her, an inch separating them. She might have been half his size, but she had other attributes.

A guard with a shoulder microphone said, "Okay, let me say this slowly so you idiots understand—get the hell out!" The other five closed the circle slightly, their movements small and deliberate.

Neither Nin nor Semo moved a muscle. No words, no expression. They'd done this a thousand times. The ending had always been the same.

The lead guard made a motion with his hand, and the circle around the Amyclaeans grew smaller again.

Semo sighed and turned to Nin, who nodded. Normal people were exhausting. There's just so much they don't know.

In a blur of movement, the two of them reduced the TransWorld guards to piles of human-shaped clothing on the floor. Sinioch's goons barely even saw them as the Amyclaeans methodically incapacitated each one. Nin didn't check to see which ones were dead and which ones were merely out cold. It hardly mattered.

When they were content that there would be no more resistance and nobody conscious to call others, Nin reached down and removed the security card from the lead guard's clip.

The Amyclaeans glided over to the elevator banks.

FORTY-NINE

Pacing helped Aeda deal with excess energy and nerves. The fact that Sinioch stood in one place, hands clasped behind his back, made her nerves even more jangly. "I tell you, this is not the time for me to leave." She walked back and forth, passing the stasis pod sitting on the floor.

He purred, "It is exactly the time. I will distract the Amyclaeans while you finish moving our … our cargo to a safer place." The more she paced, the calmer he seemed to get.

Aeda looked at Max, unconscious in the pod. "But why keep the boy here?" This stupid child had brought the Amyclaeans into their midst.

"He is safer here than in transport. The Amyclaeans cannot intrude into my private chambers. Only Armaros herself can impose upon a First Born in such a manner." Sinioch's confidence was justified, as usual. He was infallible. Their employees were not.

She took a deep breath to calm herself. "And what about the girl?" The insufferable Layil girl had been a problem for too long.

He nodded. "Should she resurface, she poses no threat. She will soon join her brother in our experiments." He crossed to where

Aeda had stopped pacing, and he turned her to face him. His hand was gentle on her cheek. "Take the cargo to Toru, as we planned. Check on the others and coordinate with the lab in Thailand. It is best for now and keeps us on our rightful path." He stroked her face, his palm on her cheekbone.

She leaned into the caress for a moment.

It was all he would allow.

FIFTY

The dark tunnels would have been almost impossible to navigate if not for Ethan's maps. After ten steps, Mara realized she needed his help and relinquished the lead to him. The glow from the screen also helped illuminate the passages, though they had been close enough to the TransWorld tower that there weren't too many twists and turns.

Eventually, they spotted a modern-looking freight elevator exactly where Ethan had predicted. As Mara reached for the UP button, a whirring noise told them the elevator was about to arrive. The five scattered and hid behind old crates piled in the passageway.

The door opened, and three burly enforcers emerged, each pushing a metallic pod on wheels into the tunnel. Two of the men returned to the elevator, leaving one with the pods.

Mara noticed right away that the pods were shaped like coffins, and her stomach sunk into her feet. "Max?" She whispered to herself and almost took a hesitant step toward them. Mick reached out and pulled her back to the shadows before the guard spotted movement.

"Hang on," Mick whispered. He waited five more seconds, until the whirring of the elevator stopped, then sneaked around to the remaining guard. The dust of a century made his footfalls silent as the grave.

When he was close enough, Mick stood up and slammed the man's head into one of the pods, knocking him senseless. The guard crumpled like a soda can.

Mick stood up and smiled, his voice still low. "Okay. Quickly and quietly now."

The other four moved around to the steel pods, and Ethan pointed to the side of one. "Look at that, it tells you age, sex, weight, heartbeat, and temperature. Kinda cool, actually." He shook his head. "No, I'm sorry. Not cool."

He peered down at the first one. "Female. 146 pounds. 35 years. 68 degrees." He smiled. "They aren't dead. Cold, yes, but not dead."

Mara felt a little bit better and scrambled as fast as she could to the next one. "Male. 168 pounds. 24 years." Her shoulders slumped.

Jackie was at the third pod. She looked at the display, then shook her head at Mara. "Nope. An old man."

Mara's anger and frustration rose, and she tried to force the door off one of the pods. She wasn't successful and didn't do any real damage. Before she could figure out how to open them, the skin on her arms began to tingle and she looked around, the pods temporarily forgotten. The sound of a door opening made all of them freeze in their tracks.

A beam of light near the elevator showed them a previously unknown stairwell, and in the doorway was framed a haggard-looking woman, barely able to stand or walk, her injuries grave and horrible. She looked out at the five of them and said, "You're here? How?"

The door slammed behind her, which made them all jump. The woman slumped to the ground.

Mick approached her. "Who the hell are you?" He took an attack stance, ready to fight in case she had a miraculous recovery.

The woman lifted her head. "I'm Elona, but it doesn't matter. I know who she is." She pointed at Mara and spoke directly to her. "Your brother is here. He's been dosed with the same drug as those poor bastards." She pointed to the pods. "And the same as me. I'm not sure what it does, but I sure as hell feel awful."

Mara rushed toward Elona, falling to her knees, her face level with the injured woman. "Where is he? Please ..."

The elevator whirred again. Elona looked up at Mara. "Lab. Twenty-fourth floor. But take the stairs." She coughed. "They're looking for me. If they see me, that'll give you time." She managed to stand up, leaning heavily on Mara.

Jackie shook her head. "Come on. If she warns anyone, we're screwed."

Mara let go of Elona, who looked at Mara with exhaustion in her face and voice. "I couldn't get Max out, so I promised him. Promised to help him." She pointed to the stairwell with a hand that looked broken in every possible way. "Go. That way."

Mara sensed she was telling the truth. First, the way Elona's presence made her skin crawl meant she was probably Offspring, too. Second, anyone as injured as she was had nothing but the truth left. Mara and Elona locked eyes. Elona nodded. Mara nodded back. "Okay, let's go. Take the stairs."

Elona pulled herself up to standing as the five of them entered the stairwell. The group began to climb as silently as they could. The last thing they heard from the tunnels was the whir of the freight elevator landing on the pad.

They didn't wait to hear who had arrived or what happened to Elona.

They already knew.

FIFTY-ONE

Nin and Semo checked every office and cubicle on the second floor of the building. They had nothing but time and a very specific job to do. As always, the Amyclaean Guards did not stop until their task was completed. Nin heard the ding of an elevator near them and decided to discontinue the work at hand until the obstruction could be handled. With one hand motion, Semo similarly stopped his search and crossed to stand next to her.

A woman in a black pantsuit approached them and bowed once. "My name is Chan, and you are Nin and Semo, our Amyclaean friends. Sinioch sends his apologies for your reception downstairs. The guards had no idea who you are." Her voice was smooth as honey and fake as a plastic rock.

Nin whispered, "Layil." She studied the face of Chan to see what clues she'd give.

"Of course. Sinioch offered any help he can to find the girl." Chan nodded and made specific eye contact with both Amyclaeans. Very specific.

Semo rasped, "Boy."

"Is the boy missing, too?" Chan acted as if she'd never heard this information before. "Well, anything in the building is yours to search. You will meet no more resistance." She bowed once again.

Semo rolled his eyes and pushed past her, continuing his work. Nin wasn't fooled, either.

Chan spoke loudly to his back, "We have nothing to hide."

Only people with hidden things said that, Nin thought.

FIFTY-TWO

The stairwell, all twenty-four floors of it, was a challenge. But Mara was fueled by the knowledge that Max was close by and had been able to ask for help from the battered woman in the Shanghai Tunnel. *He must be okay.* She repeated it over and over in her mind, the mantra soothing to the roiling in her belly.

The door from the stairwell into the building was locked with a touch screen security lock and a card swiper. Ethan extended a hand and Mara placed the TransWorld badge into it.

"If they've reset the system, it won't work. Or we'll trip an alarm ..." He hesitated for a moment.

Mara rolled her eyes, plucked the badge back out of his hand, and swiped it through the card reader. With a beep and a click, the door opened, and the screen flashed "Access Granted."

Ethan held the door open as Mick finally joined them on the landing, panting and swearing. "'Take ... the stairs,' she said." He took a couple of deep breaths. "I ... need ... a cigar."

Jackie made "stay" motions with her hands to the group in the stairwell, unsheathed her knife, and disappeared around the corner into the hall.

A crashing sound made them exchange worried glances.

She poked her head back through the door. "All clear." She smiled.

The small foyer looked like it had been bombed. A security camera hung broken and smoking from the corner, a jumble of wires hanging out from the ceiling tiles. The carpet and walls had blood smeared on them, and the door at the other end, a metal door, was firmly closed.

Jackie raised an eyebrow and shook her head. "Not my work. It was like this when I got here."

The group approached the metal door, and Mara pulled out the TransWorld security badge again. She looked at the security screen on the side of the door, craning her head around it a few times. "Uhh, there's no swiper on this one." She felt anxious butterflies in her gut ... what if Max were just on the other side of this door?

Mick and Jackie took out weapons and stood guard at the elevator. Ethan pulled out his iPad and plugged in a cable from the security system to the tablet.

The cracked screen on the iPad got Mara's attention away from dwelling on the worst. "I can't believe that thing is still working." She shook her head.

Ethan grinned at her. "I know, right?" He punched a few buttons. "Watch."

FIFTY-THREE

Chan escorted the Guards into the elevator, letting Nin and Semo enter first. Nin went to the control panel and inspected the floor numbers on the buttons. Chan was obviously lying, taking up their time while she over-explained TransWorld's business and who did what, and to whom.

They did not care.

"Most of the floors are exactly like the ones you've already seen ... offices, cubicles, storage rooms. Modern corporate life in all its glory." She smiled but made no eye contact with either of the Amyclaeans this time.

Nin saw buttons marked S1, S2, S3—perhaps subterranean floors. She raised a finger to press one of the buttons. Chan's hand snaked in front, covering the panel.

"Nothing down there but some dusty old tunnels that don't go anywhere. It's not even part of TransWorld's operation." Her voice was raised and fast. "You can certainly look later, if you want, of course." Chan nodded her head and pushed the button for 19. "But let's go through the rest of the building first. The only places Sinioch will have to show you himself are his private rooms in the penthouse. That's above my pay grade." She smiled a very nervous smile.

Nin looked at Semo, who'd raised his eyebrows. They nodded at each other.

The whole building would be inspected.

Pay grade be damned. Armaros had spoken.

Fifty-Four

Ethan managed to get the panel to unlock much faster than Mara expected. She sent him a glance of gratitude as they prepared to go beyond the steel doorway—Mick and Jackie armed to the teeth, Hiroko and Ethan behind them, and Mara trying to find a way around them.

The laboratory was fairly large and looked like an emergency room. It was obvious their test subjects were humans, or human-sized at the very least. Three stainless steel tables with IV pole attachments took up the majority of the open space, the walls covered with cabinets, and counters filled with small machines and medical supplies.

A sound caused them all to look past the exam tables, and Mara saw a stasis pod like the ones she'd seen in the tunnel. It rocked back and forth. Her heart in her throat, she cried out, "Max!" and ran to it.

Instead of her little brother, inside she saw a large, nearly naked man, his limbs contorted and bloody. An IV pumped a reddish fluid into his arm, and he was thrashing against the constraints of the walls, his eyes wild and unseeing.

Mara gasped out loud and backed away from the pod.

Hiroko and Jackie ran up next to her to look inside. Hiroko gasped, "Oh, no."

Jackie shook her head. "This is some nasty shit, but we'll find him, honey." She patted Mara on the arm, which was oddly comforting. Mara normally didn't let anyone touch her, but the events of the past few days had worn her down. She'd wanted her brother to be in the pod but was grateful he wasn't.

There was a crash as Mick sat something down hard on one of the stainless tables in the center of the lab. Everyone turned. It was a creepy looking scientist guy in a formerly white lab coat, his face held together with what looked like tape, the bloodstains on his coat turning brown.

Mick grabbed the guy by the coat lapels and pulled him close to his face. "Where is he?" He roared at the man.

The scientist sputtered a few syllables, none of which made sense. His expression was snotty and defiant, and his smirk indicated he was in want of another good beating. Mick complied by punching him in the face, which immediately broke the guy's nose and added to the stains on the lab coat. Mick raised the man up by the lapels and slammed him back down on the table. "Where. Is. He?" Mick repeated carefully into the scientist's blubbering face.

The scientist shook his head. Mick raised his hand to punch him again, but Mara leaned in before he could follow through.

"Where is Max?" she said carefully, enunciating every word.

His nose broken, his face a ruin, the scientist still managed a sneer, blood and snot everywhere. "Mr. Sinioch is—" he coughed, blood spattering onto Mara "—seeing to him personally." He coughed again, this time with a moan of pain.

The nearly naked man rattled his stasis pod as he bucked against his restraints. The scientist looked over his shoulder at the pod, then glanced back to Mara. He smiled, a deathlike mask of blood and gore. "He's waiting … for you … been waiting for a long time … your daddy and mommy, too …"

Before Mara could respond, Mick growled next to her, his fist ready to deliver a final blow to the man's simpering face. This time it was Hiroko who stopped him by pulling on his arm. He looked at her in annoyance but did as she asked.

Hiroko walked over to the table where the scientist was laying, curled up a bit to cradle his injured body. She lifted one of his feet and buckled it into the restraints, followed by the other one. The beaten man was so focused on his own pain and injuries, he didn't put up any resistance when Hiroko buckled each of his arms into a restraint.

Hiroko turned her attention to his face. "How do I save the boy?" She looked at the scientist, her face grim and deadly serious.

His response was to laugh in her face, blood bubbling up from his lips as he did. "You don't. You can't. We haven't found—" He coughed and finally realized he was tied down. He fought against the restraints.

Jackie shook her head. "Mick, kill him. Screw this bastard." Mick looked ready to comply, but Hiroko shook her head. She pushed

Mick back one step, her hands indicating the calm she wanted. She stood right next to the table and placed one hand on either side of the scientist's face. She looked him square in the eyes. Her voice changed subtly, and Mara could hear and almost see the subtle waves coming from Hiroko. "How do I save the boy?" She spoke each word carefully and slowly.

"You ... can't ..." With the last word, the scientist's body arched against the restraints, his head fighting to throw off Hiroko's hands.

Her voice still calm, her words still compelling, Hiroko repeated, "How?"

The broken man raised onto his heels, foam coming from his mouth. He couldn't escape Hiroko. "No ... please ..."

"How?" The intensity of her voice increased, and it seemed as if Hiroko had also increased the pressure on his head.

The man on the table screamed. Ethan moved next to Mara, his hand on her shoulder.

"Blood!" he screamed again. "Blood of the First Born—Sinioch's blood ..." Hiroko leaned in closer. "The drug ... it's imperfect ..." he coughed again, bloody foam speckling his lips. "Some die ... some worse ... can't control it ..." He looked over at the stasis pod, rocking on the floor.

Hiroko brought his focus back to her. "Why a child? Why this child?"

"When Armaros dies ..." He spit out blood and stared over at Mara. "It will be war ... a wonderful war ... First Borns and

Offspring ruling the world ...”

Hiroko looked stunned. “That’s ... that ... that violates everything we believe about living among humans, not over them.” The scientist gave a laugh, which he quickly choked off. “It’s against everything you believe,” he said. “But you’re wrong. Your kind, the weak kind, has always been wrong.” Then he dropped his head back and let out a yell of pain and frustration.

Mara stepped to Hiroko’s shoulder and touched her once. “We’re done. Let’s go.” Hiroko dropped her hands from the scientist’s head. She leaned against the table, her energy gone. Ethan and Mara propped her up and helped her turn to leave.

“Hang on, wait a second,” Mick said. He walked over to the stasis pod and opened it up. He yanked out a tube and unbuckled all but one restraint as the big man bucked and heaved inside.

“Sweet dreams, asshole,” Mick said to the scientist strapped to the table as they left the lab.

They could still hear his screams from the foyer outside the door.

Fifty-Five

Hiroko pointed to a red symbol on the button next to an elevator door. "That's his. Sinioch's. He's basically made a logo using the symbols of the First Born." She sighed. "You heard what he said, right?" She nodded back over her shoulder, faint shrieks still audible.

Mara shook her head. "He would've said anything to—"

Hiroko cut her off. "No. He said we need Sinioch's blood." This was as decisive and forward as Hiroko had ever been with Mara.

"So?" Mara looked at her, her eyes filled with questions.

Hiroko glared at her. "So it's not like he'll *give* you his blood. And you can't kill Sinioch—you can't do it. Even if you could, you just can't. You'd break the Covenant by killing a First Born." Her glare turned to concern again. "It's a death sentence. And it's the one thing keeping our world in check."

"Plus, we don't have that kinda firepower anyway," Mick chimed in.

Mara looked from Mick, to Hiroko, then back to Mick, who had the good grace to shrug. "You're right. You're both right. But if I need his blood ..." She shook her head. "Max is dying. Or worse."

She shuddered. Whatever it took to heal her brother and make him right again, she would do.

Ethan stepped next to Mara. "I'm going with you."

Hiroko chirped, "But you—"

Mara said at the same time, "I'm not asking you to come with me." She pushed the button to the elevator, and the doors slid open immediately.

She stepped inside and turned to look at her friends standing in the hallway.

"I can do this by myself." She nodded her head and the doors started to close.

FIFTY-SIX

When the elevator door opened, all five of them walked out and into an area not like the rest of the building. The hallway was lined with stone columns, dark and shadowy. The lighting came from the floor, with polished marble diffusing the beams shining upward. The walls were carved wood and stone, interspersed with the columns, and looked like they'd been lifted from a museum. At the far end of the hall, they saw two ornately carved wooden doors, about twice the height of a human.

"Like we would let you do this alone," Jackie said. She tsked a couple of times as she scanned the area.

Ethan cleared his throat. "Uhh, the 16th century called, and it wants its hallway back."

Mara rolled her eyes, despite herself. "Always with the joking. Even back when someone was spilling their guts in therapy." She elbowed him a little but smiled.

A shuffling sound from the end of the hall caught their ears, and they all stood at attention. Mara's hands went up, ready to grab the blades on her back. Mick and Jackie drew knives. Hiroko hid behind Ethan.

The man, and it was a large man, stepped out from the columns, his body moving in an oddly hitching manner.

Mick and Jackie walked forward slowly, the rest of the group following closely. When they were about twenty feet away, Mara looked at the man's face. "I know him." Realization dropped like a rock, and she said loudly, "You were there when they took Max!" She made a lunge forward, but Jackie held her back.

"Where's the boy?" Mick growled.

The man's head turned slightly, his eyes unfocused and blank. Drool coursed down his chin.

Mick snapped his fingers at the vacant man. "Anybody home?"

The man moved toward Mick as if he were a puppet on strings, lurching from side to side. Mick grimaced in confusion, but Mara pulled her blades from her pack.

Mick glanced at her. "Stay there." He pulled a set of spike-tipped brass knuckles from his pocket and slipped them on one hand. With the other hand, he clenched his large knife. He took a couple of steps toward the drooling guy. "Just show us where the boy is and this will go easy on you."

The man stopped his lurching advance and held up an object in his hand. It was some kind of circular blade with a handle in the middle.

At the sight of the blade, Mick charged, but the man deflected his attack, rolling from side to side, still looking like a rag doll. He twisted the circular blade, separating it into two half-circle blades—he now had one in each hand.

Hiroko screamed, which distracted Mick for a second. They turned toward the elevator and saw a hooded wraith-like figure, hands raised as if conducting a symphony. Mara realized the figure was controlling the drooling man. She spun back to see the man had slashed Mick in the back. Mick yelled out in pain but kept fighting.

Jackie tossed her knife back and forth from hand to hand, ready to take down the hooded creature. Mara nodded and stepped toward her, too. The wraith separated her hands, one controlling the drooling man, and pointed the other at Jackie.

Jackie skidded to a stop. Her eyes went wide as she realized she wasn't in control of her body anymore. Her arms shook as she raised them above her head, her knife pointed down. The wraith swung one hand down with a swish, and Jackie plunged her knife into her own belly.

"Nooooooo!" Mara screamed.

Jackie fell to the ground, her eyes on Mara as she collapsed. Hiroko ran to her.

Mara turned to the Puppeteer, clutching her blades. The creature raised her hands at Mara, but there was no effect. Mara felt nothing and continued her charge, rage coursing through her. Her blades whirled as she used every molecule of her being to perfectly execute the *gatka* training Momar had taught her. She spun and her blades hit nothing but air.

The wraith had disappeared into the shadows, then reappeared at Mara's side. She slashed at Mara with a blade. Mara felt her gauntlets respond to the metal—it was a relium blade, she was sure—but her spin had already carried her away from the Puppeteer's attack.

Out of the corner of her eye, Mara saw Mick stagger, but stay on his feet. His opponent suddenly stopped, and his blades fell from his hands. Mick finished him off with one final punch before Mara turned to face her own battle.

Ethan grabbed one of Jackie's knives from her belt and circled back behind the Puppeteer. Mara approached from the other side. The wraith was forced to stand on one of the floor lights. At the same time, Ethan and Mara charged. The Puppeteer turned suddenly to Ethan and slashed him with her blade across his chest. Mara had the opening she needed. She sunk both blades into the wraith's chest, who howled like a banshee. Mara pushed her back toward the wall, away from the bright floor light into the shadows.

The wraith vanished.

Mara stepped back into the light, her jacket covered in blood. "She's gone. Just disappeared."

She surveyed the scene. Hiroko knelt over Mick, trying her best to heal him, so much blood on and around him. Jackie was still, slumped on the marble floor. Ethan's hands were pressed to his chest wound, blood seeping between his fingers. He looked at her and said, "Go. Save. Max." As the words left his lips, he slumped to his knees.

Rage coursed through Mara's body as she strode toward the ornate double doors.

She screamed, and her power surged through her in a beam of heat.

The doors exploded into a shower of wooden shards.

The chamber inside was huge. A grand sweeping staircase dominated the right side. She assumed it was Sinioch who stood on the landing at the top of the stairs—his chest encased in armor which Mara would bet was relium.

He was dressed for battle.

Her skin under the gauntlets crawled with electricity.

At the bottom of the stairs sat a stainless-steel stasis pod, just the right size for an eleven-year-old.

Max.

She fought the pull, knowing that to go to him was a trap. Her eyes went from Sinioch to the pod and back. She shook her head and rushed to Max anyway. He was unconscious, a reddish liquid dripping into him, just like the naked man in the lab.

A smooth, oily voice broke the silence. "You will join him soon," he said, strolling down the staircase as if parading for onlookers.

Mara reached into the pod and shook Max's shoulder. "I don't know what you are and I don't care. I just want my brother back." She shook him again.

Sinioch sighed as he walked. "There is so much you don't know. I am only protecting your brother. You know I'm right, don't you? You know the others who seek to protect you actually seek to imprison you. To take what is yours. To take what is all of ours. You are powerful, Mara Layil. As were your parents. As is your kind. Let me protect you and you will never be held back again." He spoke to her like he was a benevolent uncle giving her a pony instead of the person responsible for the death of her guardian and her friends.

Another surge of anger flowed through her, her power focusing on the evil man. She pushed outward, attempting to slow time down so she could get Max out.

Nothing. A ripple passed through the air toward Sinioch, who laughed. "That's cute. Really. Playing with new powers, are we?"

Before Mara could do much more than grab her blades, Sinioch was in front of her and knocked the blades from her hands. He'd moved in a blur of speed from the bottom of the staircase—Mara hadn't even seen him until her blades hit the ground.

He sighed and looked down at her. "You could have everything. Everything you wanted." He waited for Mara to agree.

It would never happen. Never.

"Very well, child. If this is what you want." In another lightning-fast move, he grabbed her in his arms, wrapping them around her so she couldn't fight. In an instant, they were rocketing into the air, bursting through the glass dome into the sky over the penthouse.

FIFTY-SEVEN

Mara felt like she couldn't breathe. Under Sinioch's arms she saw the city lights twinkling below them. She knew this was the moment Momar had trained her for. She thought of Momar, and Max, and even her dopey, absent parents. She thought of Ethan and Mick and Jackie and Hiroko—all fighting for her and trying to help her do the right thing.

A burst of power coursed through her, rippling outward and breaking the hold Sinioch had on her. She fell back toward the earth, landing on the edge of the dome and sliding down to the roof. She felt bruised and sore, but in one piece, and she scrambled behind a piece of stonework.

Sinioch floated above the dome, his arms empty and hands on his hips. "Well, that was unexpected."

Mara felt the heat of her power again and tried to direct the burst at Sinioch. She stood up from behind the stone and flung her arms out at him, but he easily deflected it. He flicked a hand at her, and she went flying and slammed against another outcropping on the roof. Spitting blood, she tried to regain her breath, her back and ribs aching from the impact.

"You may have surprised me just then, but that will only happen once," Sinioch said in a bored voice.

If she could just freeze time again, she could get Max and get the hell out of here. She focused on her core, willing the power in her, calling it to action. To freeze a moment. To make the horrid man stop.

Nothing happened. Or nothing she could see anyway.

She tried again, her eyes scrunched up with concentration for a moment. When she opened them, he was floating just to the left of where he'd been before.

"I can see your power. I can see it when it leaves your body and I can simply step aside." He sighed. "You are becoming rather dull, Mara Layil, and I'm done playing."

"Why can't you just leave me alone? Leave my family alone. We've done nothing to you. Give me back my brother." Was it possible to reason with a madman?

No.

Her energy felt like it was drained and gone. Her body was bruised and sore, and her mouth was bleeding, probably her nose, too.

"You and your brother are an important part of my experiments. Soon I'll be able to control your powers at my will, with a snap of my fingers." He smiled at her. "Well, not your powers. You'll be dead long before we perfect the formula. But sacrifices must be made, even Offspring sacrifices."

Mara's anger surged, and with it her power was refreshed. But she didn't push it out, she internalized it this time. *Focus*. She stood and stared at him. "Dead, schmead. I'll take you out tonight rather than see my brother be one of your damn sacrifices."

Sinioch moved closer to her, still floating in space. "Don't you understand yet, infant? I cannot be killed by the likes of you." He pushed out his chest, the relium armor glowing of its own accord. "I am beyond you, Offspring. I. Am. First Born." He backed up slightly, then headed toward her at full speed, like a hawk diving for its prey.

At the same moment, Mara breathed deeply and leaped toward him, her arms extended from her body, hoping to blast a power burst at him. The gauntlets on her arms glowed like Sinioch's armor, and in the split second she jumped, long knife blades burst from the gauntlets. They extended under her hands, a part of her. She'd done nothing to make them arm themselves—she had no clue they could do something like that.

Sinioch saw the relium blades extend and looked at her in shock. He couldn't stop his momentum in time. His face contorted as he tried, and failed, to reverse his trajectory.

The impact of the two bodies colliding was like a small sonic boom. Mara's burden was lessened by the two gauntlet blades sinking firmly into Sinioch's chest through his armor. She was surprised they had penetrated his chest plate so easily, though nothing much about relium should probably surprise her anymore. She'd hated him, hated what he'd done to Max and probably her parents, but she didn't think of herself as a killer. Not really.

Then they were falling. The two crashed through the glass dome and down to the floor of the penthouse, locked together. Mara groaned as she tried to separate herself from Sinioch, the blades sunk so deeply she had trouble removing them from his body. He didn't move at all as she extricated herself. She knelt by him, her arms outstretched, blood running from the gauntlets. She looked at his body again and then to her arms. The blades morphed back into the body of the gauntlets, tight against her skin.

Sinioch's eyes fluttered open. "An Offspring? A child? How?" He took a ragged breath. "My relic?" And with one final breath, he was gone.

Mara looked around, her vision blurry as she tried to take in what had happened. Hiroko was unloading vials from the bag at her hip, siphoning up Sinioch's blood as fast as she could. She'd come into the room during the fight on the roof, and she had cuts on both arms from the falling glass. Mara staggered over to Max in the pod and took him in her arms. He was ashen, black circles under his closed eyes, his strong little muscled body a fraction of what it had been. But he was here. He was safe and still alive.

"She killed him! She killed a First Born!" A voice screeched from behind her. Mara looked up to see a woman in a black suit pointing at her. Next to her were the two Amyclaean Guards she'd tried so hard to avoid. Of course.

The guards looked at each other and moved toward Mara. One of them rasped out, "Layil. Broke Covenant." Mara had heard that phrase before, but she couldn't remember where.

Was it important?

It didn't matter. She had Max in her arms and he'd be okay again. *He has to be okay.*

FIFTY-EIGHT

The sun was just sinking into the ocean as everyone gathered for the service. Mara and Ethan stood on one side of the pyre, Max in a wheelchair next to his sister. He was bundled in a blanket, pale and weak, but he held Mara's hand with just enough strength to make her smile. Hiroko held his other hand firmly, staying in constant contact with him.

Momar lay in state on the pyre. His black turban was immaculate; his blades crossed over his chest. A black wool shawl covered his torso, ornate embroidery on every inch.

Abbot Greb and a few other monks were near the pyre, while the two Amyclaean Guards stood like stone sentries behind Mara. She had a feeling they would never let her out of their sight again.

A roar of deep-throated motorcycles approached the group, and they watched as the bikes parked and their passengers walked over. Mick leaned on a cane and Strabler helped him cross the short distance to the pyre. He stood in front of Mara, who dropped Max's hand for a moment to give Mick a gentle hug. Mick laughed a little and released her. He walked to the pyre and nestled a bottle of Laphroaig single malt Scotch between the pieces of wood.

"For Jackie," he said, clearing his throat.

When the gathering was complete, Abbot Greb pulled a burning torch from the sand and walked over to Mara. He handed her the torch with a nod. She accepted it and touched it to the pyre, which lit at once.

Ethan stepped forward to help her back. She nodded her head and returned to Max's side.

The monks released paper sky lanterns into the night, the delicate rice paper glowing from the small flame inside. The lights floated out over the Pacific Ocean, as the monks sang a somber and beautiful chant to the Scribe, while Mara ignored the tears on her cheeks. It was a lovely and fitting service for Momar. He would have loved it and been embarrassed at the attention.

Mara felt a tap on her shoulder and turned to see the abbot waiting for her. She nodded and stepped forward. He spoke quietly into her ear, something only she could hear. There would be repercussions. There would be inquiries. Who knew if she'd ever see the light of day again?

Her expression without emotion, she nodded again, very slowly.

No matter what the abbot and the Amyclaean Guards had in store for her, she wasn't going to give up. There were still people out to harm her family. It didn't matter where they put her or what they did, she wouldn't rest until her people were safe. And she'd do whatever was needed to keep them that way.

She was Mara Layil and she was going to keep fighting.

She was Offspring.

AFTERWORD

Aeda knelt by Sinioch's side at the bier, the royal purple cloth covering him stitched with her own hands and anointed with an ocean of her tears. Moonlight was the only illumination in the room, the darkness perfectly fitting her mood. The Layil girl had killed her love. Killed her dreams.

Aeda's heart had been torn from her, her life had been torn from her, and her world had been torn apart. But the black granite slab holding Sinioch's body was perfect. His suit was perfect.

And her revenge would be perfect.

The Hunt for Mara Layil, book two in the Angel Punk Saga trilogy, is available now at angelpunksaga.com.

ACKNOWLEDGMENTS

Like all good things, the Angel Punk Saga is possible only through the hard work and support of many people.

First, to Julie O'Connell who adapted the Angel Punk screenplay into the book you're now reading. You jumped right into this existing world and helped us bring it to others.

To Amber J. Keyser, author of *The Hunt for Mara Layil*, for all you have done to bring Mara and the rest of the characters in this saga to life. Your love and care for the story and people in this world shines through your words on the page.

Without the original concept and ongoing dedication of Devon Lyon, Kevin Curry and Scott Bernard Nelson, none of this would have been possible. Sometimes crazy ideas come together to create new worlds!

Huge shout out to Eric Doebele, Jack Phan, Jake Rossman, Chris Weilert, and Matthew Wilson for being early believers in this story and project. All of your help and support over the years manufacturing inertia has been invaluable.

Jennifer Stangel's work navigating the complexities of the publishing world is the reason you're holding this book or reading it on your electronic device. For that and being a believer in the project from the beginning, she gets eternal gratitude.

For the investors in the Angel Punk Saga, without you this would have never gotten off the ground. Thank you, thank you, thank you.

A hearty 'Huzzah!' goes out to the book cover artists, Steven Barker and Amelia Harp, for bringing their unique visions of the world to life.

To Shannon Wheeler for his generosity in sharing knowledge about the comic and publishing world, we offer a toast of rich, black coffee. And Levi Moroshan for believing in the project and bringing his photo talents to the table so many times.

A special thanks to the Angel Punk comic art team who brought Mara and the rest of the characters to life visually, including Val Mayerik, Bob Wiacek, Steve Olliff, Brian Snoddy and Tom Orzechowski. Also, our art team intern Sarah Cloutier added so many incredible images to this world.

About the Author

Manuscript by Julie O'Connell

Visit angelpunksaga.com for author and creators' biographies. Want to learn even more about the hidden supernatural world of Angel Punk? Then be sure to also visit the website's blog and art pages for additional, in-depth material, a free short story, and a downloadable PDF of chapter one from both Offspring (book one) and The Hunt for Mara Layil (book two).